Match Wits with The Hardy Boys®!

Collect the Original
Hardy Boys Mystery Stories®
by Franklin W. Dixon

Celebrate 60 Years with the World's Greatest Super Sleuths!

THE CLUE IN THE EMBERS

Tony Prito enlists the help of his detective friends Frank and Joe Hardy when a sinister stranger demands that Tony sell him the bizarre curio collection he has just inherited.

While the boys are discussing this suspicious incident, the stranger, Valez, telephones and threatens Tony. That same afternoon the three boys collect the cases of curios at a freight station. On their way back to Tony's house an attempt is made on Joe's life. The next day a red-haired seaman claims that two medallions in the collection are his. But the medallions are missing! Did Valez steal them? And what was their significance?

Unraveling the clues in this exciting mystery takes the Hardys and their friends to a desolate region in Guatemala and straight into the hands of a gang of dangerous thugs.

"We're trapped!" cried Chet

The Hardy Boys Mystery Stories®

THE CLUE
IN THE EMBERS

BY

FRANKLIN W. DIXON

GROSSET & DUNLAP
Publishers • New York
A member of The Putnam & Grosset Group

PRINTED ON RECYCLED PAPER

CONTENTS

THE CLUE
IN THE EMBERS

CHAPTER I

A Strange Inheritance

THE shrill ringing of the Hardy telephone greeted Frank and Joe as they swung into the driveway after a preseason football practice at the Bayport High field.

"Hurry!" Mrs. Hardy called a moment later. "This is the third time Tony Prito has phoned!"

"Must be important," said blond, seventeen-year-old Joe to his brother Frank, dark-haired and a year older. "Be right there, Mom!"

Clearing the porch steps in two strides, Joe hurried in to the phone. "Hello, Tony. What's up?"

"How would you and Frank like to see some shrunken heads?"

"See what?"

"Six shrunken human heads!"

"Where are they?"

"I've inherited a lot of mysterious curios from

my uncle Roberto," Tony replied excitedly. "He had a shop full of them in New York when he died. The shipment, including the shrunken heads, will arrive at the railroad station here at one-forty this afternoon."

"And you need our muscle to help you load and unload?" Joe asked with a chuckle.

"Right. But what's more important, I've received a strange telegram in connection with this stuff. I'll show it to you when you get here."

"Sounds like a new mystery. Wait till I tell Frank! Well, we'll be at your house around one."

Joe hung up and told his brother about their appointment with Tony. He had not quite finished when Mrs. Hardy came in.

"What's this about a mystery?" the slender, attractive woman asked.

The boys related the story.

"You're both just like Dad," their mother said with a smile.

Fenton Hardy, an internationally famous detective, had served many years with the New York City police force. Later he had settled in Bayport, a bustling seaport of fifty thousand inhabitants. From his big house at Elm and High streets he carried on a busy practice as a private investigator. His sons were following in his footsteps. The first case they had solved was *The Tower Treasure,* and their latest one was *The Hooded Hawk Mystery.*

"I'll sure need some nourishment if I'm going to hassle with a lot of shrunken heads," Frank declared. "Joe, let's finish that clam chowder Mother made yesterday."

"It sure was good." Joe laughed. "Chet ate three bowls of it while he was here."

Chet Morton was the Hardys' chubby pal who often went along with them to follow up clues. He lived on a farm about a mile from Bayport.

"Shall we phone Chet and ask him to come to the station?" Joe asked.

"I'm sure Tony called him already," Frank replied.

Within ten minutes the boys were on their way to Tony's house. They found their friend sitting on the front steps. One of the Prito Construction Company's large trucks was parked at the curb. Tony waved anxiously at the boys.

"Now what's this all about?" Frank asked.

"Somebody wants to buy the curio collection sight unseen."

"That's strange," Joe commented.

"Look," Tony said, reaching into his pocket. "Here's the telegram I got."

Signed with the single name Valez, the message was an offer to buy, for two hundred dollars, the entire collection of curios.

"This arrived yesterday," Tony explained. "And notice that Valez, whoever he is, says he's going to phone this afternoon and make arrangements to pick up the stuff."

Suspicious, the Hardys glanced at each other. Frank suggested that the collection might be worth much more than two hundred dollars.

"Sure," said Joe. "I wouldn't take his offer."

"Right," Frank continued. "Valez is too eager to make a deal. Besides, I think he has a nerve to assume you're going to sell him the curios before you've had a chance to have them appraised."

"Do you have a list of all the things, Tony?" Joe asked.

"No, not a complete one," Tony replied, "but this letter from the estate's executor, a bank in New York City, mentions several of the items."

The boys scanned the paragraph that told of the curios.

"Look!" Joe exclaimed. "You even have four Moorish scimitars!"

"What about them?" Tony asked.

Frank, who had done some research on swords in connection with a previous mystery, explained that a scimitar is a crescent-shaped saber used originally by Moorish horsemen, and still popular during the Wars of Napoleon. Made of fine Damascus steel, often with guards of gold set with precious stones, these antique weapons are rare and valuable.

"And see here," Frank continued. "The shrunken heads are mentioned, too."

These heads, or tsanstas, the letter explained, have a considerable value in the souvenir market, despite laws against their sale or barter.

"The Andean Indians used to take the heads of their enemies in local warfare," Joe said. "I read up on this once. The skull was removed from the severed head and boiled until it was reduced to the size of a man's fist. Then the eyes were pinned and laced, and the inside treated with hot stones and sand. Through the use of a local herb, the hair remained long and kept its original luster."

"Pretty savage," Tony remarked.

"Well, we'd better head for the station," Frank urged. "The train's about due."

Just then the phone in the Prito hallway rang.

"Maybe it's Valez," Tony said and ran inside. Frank and Joe followed.

Tony picked up the phone and listened. His jaw tightened. For several seconds the three boys stood still while the high-pitched voice on the other end chattered without a pause.

Tony indicated to the Hardys that it was Valez. Then he said, "No. I'm sorry, but I'm not interested in your offer. Thanks just the same."

Valez's voice grew loud and angry.

"I'm not selling at this point," Tony said firmly.

The Hardys heard Valez snap one more remark as Tony hung up.

"What did he say?" Frank asked.

"He threatened me," Tony replied. "Said I'd be sorry. And he's right here in Bayport!"

"Wow!" Joe exploded. "We'd better get down to the station. He might try to pull a fast one."

"I'm glad you fellows are coming along," Tony said as they went out of the house. "I called Chet, but he couldn't make it."

The train had not yet arrived when the boys reached the terminal.

"According to Valez's accent he's definitely Spanish," Tony said. "I imagine him to be the small, excitable kind."

They glanced around the platform, but no Spanish-looking man was in sight.

"Here comes the train," Frank said.

They watched the freight agent run his cart to a boxcar. The door opened. Crates and cartons were quickly lifted out.

"They're all yours," the agent told Tony.

Joe whistled. "Some haul," he said as box after box, some with strange, foreign-looking markings, was piled high onto the cart. The trio watched alertly out of the corners of their eyes for the sudden appearance of any particularly interested person.

"Okay, Tony!" the agent said at last, and handed him the bill of lading to be signed.

Without losing a moment, the three boys helped pull the cart to the truck and started loading the cases onto it. Working feverishly to finish the job

"They're all yours," the agent told Tony

so they could get home and examine the curios, they were glad to have the help of two friends whom they had spotted on the platform.

As Joe lifted the last case onto the truck, he said, "Frank, you sit up front with Tony. I'd like to stay back here and act as a lookout."

"Okay," his brother agreed as their two friends waved good-by. He jumped into the cab. Tony climbed to the driver's seat and started the motor. Seconds later they were on their way to the Prito house.

Sitting atop one of the cases in the open back of the truck, Joe had a good view of the station and the public square. "Still no sign of action from Valez," he mused. "I wonder if the whole business was just a hoax."

Frank was thinking along the same line. As they turned into the tree-lined avenue two blocks from the Prito home, he let out a sigh of relief. "It seems our buddy gave up on us," he said.

But Tony did not share his optimism. "Maybe he's just biding his time."

"Let's see if Joe noticed anything," Frank said, and slid back the glass panel in the rear of the cab. "Joe," he called out, "this job turned out to be a lot easier than I expected. Anything new on your end?"

Joe was about to answer, when he caught sight of an arrowhead-like missile streaking through the air directly toward him!

CHAPTER II

A Stolen Curio

SEEING the missile whizzing toward him, Joe ducked, but he felt a stinging blow on his right arm.

"Stop!" he yelled to Tony. "Get that fellow! He shot at me!" Joe pointed to a man who had dodged from behind a tree and was now running away at top speed.

The vehicle lurched to a halt. Frank flung open the cab door and raced toward a wooded stretch beyond the sidewalk.

"Watch it!" Joe called after his brother. "That guy's got a blowgun!"

Frank pursued the assailant into the woods and disappeared.

Meanwhile, Tony eased the truck to the edge of the road. He turned to see what had happened to Joe. "Something hit you?" he asked.

"Yes." Joe showed a small arrowhead which he

had picked up from the floor. A tiny paper was glued to its base. Without taking the time to examine either, Joe thrust them into his pocket. He told Tony to guard the truck, and dashed off in search of his assailant.

He sprinted a hundred yards into the woods. Thrashing through a stretch of thicket, he called, "Frank! Where are you?"

"Over here!" Frank was standing near a wire fence that enclosed two closely spaced factory buildings.

"He jumped the fence," Frank panted as Joe came up to him. "Took off between the two plants. We'll never catch him now!"

"Let's get back to the truck," Joe suggested. "This attack might have been a ruse to lure us away!"

They hurried toward the street. To their relief, the truck was still there.

"Did you get a good look at the man?" Tony asked.

"Not too good," Frank replied. "He's short, thin, dark, and I think he's got a small mustache."

Joe frowned. "How old do you think he is?"

Frank shrugged. "Whatever his age, he's very wiry. You should have seen him vault that fence!"

"Joe, you'd better sit up front with us now," Tony said. "We can't afford to let that guy take any more pot shots at you."

Once inside the cab, the boys examined the

lead arrowhead and the paper covering its base. A message was scrawled in barely legible script, warning Tony not to dispose of the curios.

"First Valez wants me to sell the stuff, and now he tells me not to or I'll get in trouble!" Tony exclaimed.

"You're jumping to a conclusion," Frank objected. "We don't really have any proof that this man was Valez."

"That's right," Joe said. "There's a good chance that someone else is after your curios."

Tony sighed. "Looks as if we have a full-fledged mystery on our hands."

Joe changed the subject. "Tony, what are you going to do with all these things?" he asked.

"Put them in the garage for the time being. I can't think of where else to store them."

"I'm not so sure that it is the safest place," Frank commented.

"I have an idea," Joe said. "Why don't you ask the new Howard Museum to take care of them? Maybe you can give them some of the pieces and see if Mr. Scath will store the rest in return."

"Good thinking," Frank agreed.

"Okay," Tony said. "I'll give him a ring."

Soon the trio arrived at the Prito home. Tony parked the truck, and while the Hardy boys guarded the shipment, he went inside and phoned Mr. Scath.

"The museum is open late tonight," said the

curator. "I suggest that you bring your curios around about nine o'clock, after closing time. There won't be anybody in the building and I'll have a chance to look at them."

As Tony stepped into the yard he was startled to see a man tiptoeing along the side of the garage. He was short and wore a felt hat pulled low.

Tony yelled. The intruder took off like a streak of lightning. Tony chased him down the block, but he escaped in a car.

Frank and Joe had heard Tony call out. "I'll go, you stay with the truck," Frank said and ran after Tony. They met in the street.

"What was that all about?" Frank asked.

"A guy was sneaking around our garage. Probably Valez. Too bad I couldn't catch him. He drove off."

The boys were worried when they talked things over with Joe. "That guy means business!" Joe declared. "We'd better keep a lookout." They took turns keeping watch as they inspected the curios in the garage.

Tony found a pair of old Indian clubs and started swinging them. Joe pulled out a small stuffed alligator of little value. But in the same box was a set of rare old travel books from the sixteenth century. Another interesting find was a small chest filled with old silver pieces.

"Probably belonged to some pirate," Joe remarked, while Frank stacked four scimitars on a wall rack.

As time passed, one thing became certain: the collection was worth much more than two hundred dollars.

"Do you realize what time it is?" Frank asked hours later. "Almost six-thirty. And I'm starved!"

"My folks won't be home for dinner," Tony said. "Why don't you call your mother and tell her you'll eat here?"

"Great idea!" Joe said. "I'll phone."

He went into the house while Tony padlocked the garage doors. A few minutes later the three boys met in the kitchen.

"And now for some food!" said Tony. Soon he had a large pot of spaghetti cooking on the stove. "My mother made a lot of good meat sauce to go with this," he said. "And there's homemade apple pie for dessert."

The boys took their time eating and were deep in conversation when Frank suddenly interrupted. "Sh-h!"

"What's the matter?" Tony asked.

"I heard a noise coming from the garage!"

They were silent and listened tensely. Then Joe got up and walked to the window. He peered out, then shrugged. "Nobody outside," he said.

Frank was not convinced. "We'd better have a look," he said.

The boys went out. Seeing that the garage was still padlocked, they ran around to the rear. The window was wide open!

"Take it easy," Tony warned as Joe leaped onto the ledge and climbed in. Frank followed.

Tony walked around front again, opened the padlock, and entered the garage through the door. No one was inside but Frank and Joe.

Quickly the trio checked the crates. Nothing seemed to be disturbed. Suddenly Frank's eyes focused on the wall rack.

"One of the scimitars is missing!" he exclaimed.

CHAPTER III

Fire in the Mummy Case

DISMAYED, the boys saw that only three of the Moorish swords remained in the rack. Frank and Joe dashed outside and made a quick search through the neighborhood. They found no trace of the burglar.

In disgust they went back to Tony's house and told him of their failure.

"It's all my fault," Frank said grimly. "I should have put the swords back into the crate."

"Look, don't worry about it," Tony said. "Let's wash the dishes and then load the truck before something else happens."

They had almost finished cleaning up the kitchen when the doorbell rang. Could it be Valez again?

"Joe, keep an eye on the garage from the window," Tony said. "I'll answer the bell and Frank can help me in case of trouble."

The tension was broken when Tony opened the door. The caller was the boys' chubby friend Chet Morton.

"Did I just miss a meal?" Chet chuckled when Frank appeared from behind the door, still holding a dish towel.

"You did." Frank laughed. "But you're just in time to help us load about twenty crates onto Tony's truck."

Chet groaned and slumped into a chair. "Okay," he said. "I walked right into your trap. I'll carry the little ones." Then he added, "But tell me what this is all about."

After giving him a brief account, the boys started the job. As darkness began to settle, Tony confided in Frank that he would feel better with police protection.

Frank agreed. "Let's call Chief Collig. He'll be at headquarters now. He doesn't go off duty until late in the evening."

Tony phoned and told the chief what had taken place during the day.

"Seems as if you've got some serious trouble on your hands," Collig said after he heard about the attack on Joe. "I'll send a patrol car over to escort you to the museum. And keep me posted if anything else happens."

"Will do," Tony promised. "And thanks, Chief."

The four boys worked quickly to have the truck loaded before the arrival of the police car.

"Here it comes!" Joe called as Tony swung the last crate into position.

The squad car pulled over to the curb and the policeman called out to the boys. "Ready?"

"Right," Tony replied.

"I'll go ahead, and you follow. Honk if you have any trouble in the back."

"Okay."

Tony backed the truck into the street. "Anyone who tries to play games this time will get a hot reception," he remarked.

On the way to the Howard Museum, the boys talked about the possible dangers that faced them. Tony recalled Valez's angry threat and wondered if even the police escort would stop the man from attempting a robbery.

"I'd hate to meet a guy with a blowgun out here," Chet said with a shiver. "He could hide in the bushes. It's mighty eerie in this area."

Minutes later the patrol car swung to the right and entered the curving, dimly lighted driveway of the ivy-covered museum. As the truck followed, all eyes searched the shrubbery surrounding the building. But there was no sign of anyone lying in wait.

Tony grunted in relief. "Boy, am I glad that's over!"

The massive door creaked open and the slender figure of the curator appeared. Mr. Scath hurried down the steps and greeted the boys, then told them to move the crates into the basement.

"Let's hurry," Tony urged. "The sooner we get this stuff behind that door, the better I'll feel."

As the four lugged the boxes from the truck, the officer kept an alert watch for Tony's enemy. For fifteen minutes the tense operation continued. Finally Joe picked up the last crate and called to the policeman that the job was finished.

The officer smiled. "In case you run into any more trouble, just call us," he said and drove off.

Mr. Scath bolted the big door and accompanied the boys to the basement. His eyes flashed with excitement.

"I can hardly wait to make a careful study of these pieces," he said. "From what you told me, Tony, there might be some real treasures here."

Tony nodded thoughtfully. "I sure appreciate your help, Mr. Scath," he said. "And if you can give me an appraisal, I'll know what the collection is worth."

The curator opened one of the crates and pulled out a few items. "Some things," he said, "won't amount to anything, of course. Like this box, for instance."

He examined an object that looked like an ordinary cigarette box. It was about four inches long and was made of dark wood, with a sign painted on it in yellow.

He was just about to toss it back into the crate when Frank stopped him. "If Tony doesn't want it," he said, "I'll take it. I like the design."

"Help yourself," Tony said.

"Well," the curator said, "it's getting late. Come back some other time and we'll check everything out. Okay?"

"Any time you say," Tony replied.

Mr. Scath walked to the door and beckoned the boys to precede him. Then he locked up. Joe led the way upstairs to the main hall.

Suddenly he stopped short. He held out his hand for silence and gazed toward the room where a mummy and several sarcophagi were on display.

"Mr. Scath," he said in a low voice, "is anyone working in the building?"

"No," the curator assured him. "Nobody's here except us."

"Sh-h!" Joe warned.

A sharp scraping noise came from the mummy room. A muffled sound followed.

As Mr. Scath switched on all the hall lights, the Hardys, Chet, and Tony ran toward the room. Frank stopped at the door, flicked the light switch, and quickly surveyed the pillared exhibition hall. There was no sign of an intruder.

"There must be someone in the museum!" Mr. Scath whispered nervously. "Quick! One of you inspect upstairs. The rest search this floor!"

Chet, nearest to the spiral steps, gripped the iron rail and started up. Frank and Joe dashed to the left of the Egyptian Room. Mr. Scath and Tony headed through the middle of the hall.

"What a spooky place!" Joe exclaimed in hushed tones to his brother. He was looking into an open sarcophagus and saw the painted face of the mummy which lay in an inner coffin.

"Don't worry about the spooks!" Frank replied. "But do you smell smoke?" he asked, sniffing.

"I sure do," Joe answered, alarmed.

A strong odor of smoke soon filled their nostrils. It was hard to tell where it was coming from, but both boys dashed among the sarcophagi to locate its source.

"Here it is!" Joe cried out a moment later. "Mr. Scath, Frank—come here quick!"

As the curator appeared in the aisle, followed by Frank and Tony, Joe pointed to a slightly opened, ornately designed sarcophagus. Gray-white smoke was pouring from it.

"Give me a hand!" Mr. Scath cried. "Lift up the cover!"

Tony and Joe put their shoulders against the lid and forced it upward. The smoke thinned into a column, exposing, atop the coffin inside, a cone-shaped pile of embers!

Frank took off his sports shirt and smothered the glow that remained in the embers.

"Whoever made this fire must still be in the building!" Mr. Scath warned. "No one could get in or out of here without the keys that I have in my pocket. That means someone must have hidden in here before nine o'clock."

"Say!" Joe exclaimed. "Wonder if Chet's found out anything." He called out, but there was no reply from the second floor.

"We'll search the entire building for the intruder," Mr. Scath said grimly. "He can't get away. We'll start in the basement."

The Hardys, worried about Chet's failure to answer, decided that one of them should run upstairs to check on their friend.

"I'll go," Frank volunteered. "Joe, you help Mr. Scath and Tony." Frank headed for the same staircase that Chet had taken.

As the others were about to go down to the basement, Mr. Scath decided to remove the embers from the sarcophagus. "There's too much danger of their containing a spark or two. Wait here."

The curator got a small shovel and an empty metal wastebasket from his office and returned to the sarcophagus. He was about to drop the ashes into the basket when Joe suddenly stopped him.

"Mr. Scath, I'd like to take the ashes to our lab to study them."

"Certainly," the curator agreed. "Mighty good idea." He had heard of the modern, fully equipped, crime-detection laboratory that the

Hardys had set up on the second floor of their garage.

Joe got a museum specimen envelope and the curator carefully poured a large sample of the ashes and charred remains into it. Joe sealed the envelope and slipped it into his pocket.

"Now let's find the intruder!" Mr. Scath urged, and the trio headed for the basement.

Suddenly, from the second floor, came a crash and a bloodcurdling shriek!

CHAPTER IV

Skylight Escape

ELECTRIFIED by the piercing outcry from upstairs, Joe and Tony dashed up the spiral stairway. Mr. Scath followed as quickly as he could.

Frank had already reached Chet, who admitted yelling. He said he had not heard Joe calling him. "B-but I wish I had," he added, slowly getting to his feet and leaning against the wall opposite the American Indian Gallery. His face was white and he rubbed the side of his head.

"When I looked into the American Indian hall I saw that figure start to move!" He pointed to the tall statue of a Cherokee chieftain lying across the passageway.

"What?" Joe asked.

"It walked!" Chet insisted. "Then suddenly it toppled over."

"No doubt the intruder moved it!" Scath said.

"Right," Chet said. "When it fell over, it hit

me on the side of my head. It knocked me down and the guy got away!"

"He can't be far," Frank said grimly. "Let's keep looking!"

The search continued for half an hour. Methodically the group went from top to bottom of the museum. There were no windows on the first floor, and those on the second floor were locked.

"I'd better call the police," Mr. Scath finally decided.

But Frank was reluctant to admit defeat yet. "If every door and window is locked, I want to find out how that intruder got away."

"How about the skylight?" Joe suggested.

"There's just the one in the prints gallery on the top floor," Mr. Scath answered. "I never thought of that. It's not fitted with a special lock!"

Frank and Joe went up to the third floor and looked at the skylight. It was open!

"The intruder went across the roof and down the ivy vines," Joe said.

Frank nodded. "No doubt. We don't have a chance of catching up with him now."

The Hardys returned to the second floor and told Mr. Scath of their discovery. The curator explained that the skylight was checked every evening at closing time. "Obviously the intruder must have hidden in the museum before the staff left," he concluded. "Well, we've done all we can. Better get some sleep," he advised. "We can discuss the mystery another time."

"Did you report this incident to Chief Collig?" Frank asked.

"Yes. I told him you were out here working on it."

"Maybe when we analyze the ashes from the fire in the sarcophagus we'll find a clue," Joe said.

After Frank climbed up and locked the skylight, the group headed for the ground floor. Mr. Scath asked if Tony would mind following his car in the truck. "With all the odd things going on around here tonight, I don't feel much like driving home alone," he said.

Joe offered to ride with the curator. Tony would follow. The car moved slowly along the driveway and turned into the main road.

Its two passengers rode for a couple of blocks in silence. Then Joe remembered the arrowhead that had been fired at him from the blowgun earlier that day. It was still in his pocket. He pulled it out.

"Mr. Scath," he said when the curator stopped for a red light, "do you know what country this comes from?"

Scath picked up the object from Joe's palm. He examined it carefully. "Hm! I have never seen one quite like this before," he said slowly.

"Where would you guess it's from?" Joe prodded.

"That would be hard to say," Scath replied. "Could be from South America. But I can't be sure."

Joe slipped the arrowhead back into his pocket. After getting out at Mr. Scath's home, he stepped up into the truck. On the way to Chet's house he told his brother about his conversation with the curator.

"Maybe that's where Valez is from," Frank said thoughtfully.

Tony dropped Chet off, then the Hardys.

"Let us know if you hear from Valez again," Frank called as he drove off.

The boys went upstairs to their bedroom. Joe noticed it was past midnight. Then he eyed Frank, who stood in the middle of the room, lost in thought.

"Hey, for a fellow who's been on the go since eight o'clock yesterday morning, you don't seem very sleepy, Frank!" he said.

"I'm not. Why don't we analyze those ashes you sampled?"

Joe yawned. "Okay. But let's try not to wake up Mother. She'll think we're crazy to work so late."

The boys removed their shoes, put on moccasins, and headed for the laboratory.

"Set up the microtome," Frank suggested. "I'll get the photomicrograph ready."

Joe shook out the contents of the envelope and

selected one of the firmer tiny charred pieces. He clamped this in place on the microtome. Then, running a finely honed knife blade delicately through it, Joe cut off a section.

"What thickness?" he asked.

"About two thousandths of an inch," Frank replied.

Working carefully, Joe cut other tissue-thin sections from several angles, letting them drop onto a glass slide. In a few moments Frank had prepared several photomicrographs of them, showing distinct wood grains.

"Now we'll see what was burning in the sarcophagus," Frank said as he prepared to project the first lantern slide.

The enlarged curves in the picture revealed clear patterns. Frank compared them with a chart in an encyclopedia.

"The grain matches the mahogany," he said. The boys examined the pattern again and compared it with further angle shots. "It's Central American mahogany!" Frank concluded. "And Valez could be from there!"

"And the arrowhead!" Joe added. "It all points to Central and South America!"

"First thing tomorrow we'll airmail that arrowhead to Dad's friend Mr. Hopewell in Chicago," Frank decided. "He'll be able to identify it. He's a specialist in primitive weapons."

After storing the packet of ashes and the lantern

slides in their small safe, the boys tiptoed back to their bedroom. A few moments later they were sleeping soundly.

In the morning Joe woke up first. "Hm! I smell bacon and eggs," he said and jumped out of bed.

Fifteen minutes later both brothers were in the kitchen, saying good morning to their Aunt Gertrude, Mr. Hardy's tall, angular sister, who stood at the stove.

Presently their mother joined them and they all sat down at the dining-room table.

"What are you two up to now?" Aunt Gertrude asked as she passed bacon and buns.

Frank gave an account of the curios, the missile, the chase, and the events at the museum.

"Too bad your father's out of town," Mrs. Hardy remarked. "I'm sure he'd be interested in this." Then, with a note of anxiety in her voice, she added, "Please be careful. Especially of this man who walks around with a blowgun!"

"Don't worry, Mom," Frank said. "We'll be on guard every minute."

Breakfast was almost over when the telephone rang.

"Might be Fenton," Aunt Gertrude suggested.

"Or Mr. Scath," Frank said.

"I'll get it," Joe offered, pushing back his chair. He disappeared and picked up the phone. "Hello."

"Joe," replied the excited voice of Tony Prito, "Valez just phoned again."

"Boy! He doesn't waste any time, does he? What did he say?"

"He made threats against Frank and you!"

CHAPTER V

Missing Valuables

"Valez threatened us?" Joe exclaimed. "Why, Tony?"

"He says that you're interfering with my selling him the collection. I told him you had nothing to do with it. I wouldn't sell it, anyway. Boy, was he mad! Told me in no uncertain terms that if I didn't give him what he wanted and you guys didn't keep out of this deal he'd get all of us!"

"Wonder how Valez knows that we're friends," Joe asked.

"He must have found out somehow. Called you those Hardy boys."

When Frank heard about the threat he began to speculate about what to do next.

"Now listen to me!" Aunt Gertrude interrupted. "You'd better pay attention to that warning. There's no sense in waiting until danger's right on top of you."

The front doorbell sounded and the lecture ended. A tall, broad-shouldered stranger with red hair was standing on the porch. Several tattoo marks covered his thick bared forearms.

"Good morning," Frank said politely.

"Are you one of the Hardy boys?"

"Yes."

"My name is Willie Wortman," the man began in a voice that seemed no less friendly than his handshake. "I'm from New York."

"Did you arrive here this morning?" Joe asked as they entered the living room. Frank swung a chair around for the caller.

"Yes."

Wortman explained that he was a seaman on a freighter plying to Central and South America. At the mention of these last words Joe and Frank exchanged glances.

"Well," Wortman continued, "my ship docked in New York last week. After I was paid off, I went to visit an old shopkeeper friend of mine—a man named Roberto Prito."

"Prito!" Frank exclaimed.

"Yes," Wortman went on. "But my friend had died and his shop was locked tight. I sure felt bad. He was a good guy." After a pause the sailor continued. "I was disappointed, too, because I'd hoped to pick up two medallions there—one the size of a half dollar, the other somewhat larger.

"I heard from a neighbor of Roberto that a

large shipment of objects from the shop had been sent to Tony Prito here in Bayport. Figuring the medallions might have been in the shipment, I came on out. I went to Tony's house as soon as I got into town. He says he's pretty sure they're not in the collection. Tony had to take the truck out on a rush job for his dad, so he advised me to come here and talk to you about them."

"Did those two medallions belong to you?" Frank asked.

"Yes," Wortman replied. "I got them from a buddy who has since been killed. A short time ago, when I was broke, I hocked them with Roberto."

"And you're trying to buy them back?" Frank asked.

"Y-yes." His halting reply puzzled the boys. Wortman went on, "I guess I may be a bit foolish about going to such trouble to locate them. I'd just like to get hold of them for the sake of senti-ment—something to remember my friend by."

"What do the medallions look like?" Frank asked.

Wortman explained that the medallions were made of some cheap metal, and had a design of curving lines. In addition, the larger one had a fake opal set in it, while the other had the word *Texichapi* inscribed on it.

"What does that mean?" Joe asked.

"I don't know," the seaman replied.

"We went through the whole shipment," Frank said, "and I'm positive the medallions are not part of it. But we'll look again. If we find them, you'll have to make arrangements with Tony."

"That's fair enough," the visitor replied. "Here's where you can contact me." He handed Frank a piece of paper with a New York address. Then he rose from his chair, thanked the boys, and started for the door. Suddenly he stopped short.

"There's one more thing," he said. "I was told in a seaport down in Central America that there's a curse connected with those medallions."

"A curse!" Joe exclaimed.

"Right. Trouble will come to anyone who sells these objects. That's the real reason why I want to get them back."

The boys accompanied Wortman to the front door, then returned to the dining room to finish their breakfast. They discussed the sailor's strange story.

"Do you think he was telling the truth?" Joe asked his brother.

"I think the part about the curse was trumped up," Frank replied. "His imagination probably got the better of him. But the rest sounds real enough."

"Let's ask Mr. Cosgrove at the New York bank who's acting as executor of Prito's will if he's come across the medallions."

"I'll call Tony and ask him to get in touch with him," Frank said.

Later that morning Tony called back, saying that Mr. Cosgrove had no record of the two medallions.

Where could they be? What had Roberto Prito done with them? Had he sold them, or was Wortman's story a fake?

Their discussion was interrupted by a long-distance call from Mr. Hardy. He was in New York City. He told his sons news of general interest about his latest case, then said, "I was offered an assignment that sounded intriguing, but I had to turn it down because I'm too busy. Upon the recommendation of a detective agency here, a man by the name of Alberto Torres called on me at my hotel."

"Who's he?" Frank asked.

"He claimed to be the head of a Guatemalan patriotic society," his father explained. "He says his group is trying to uncover a treasure of antiquity. They don't know where it is, but suspect that its location is known to some unscrupulous people who are trying to steal it. Naturally, the treasure belongs to the government."

"Maybe we could work on it until you'd be ready to take over," Frank suggested. "Did Torres have any idea where it is at all?"

"He said that their only lead is a couple of

medallions which have disappeared," Mr. Hardy answered.

"Medallions!" Frank exclaimed, and quickly related what had happened in the detective's absence. Mr. Hardy listened intently and told Frank that he would try at once to contact Torres.

"Hang up," he said, "and I'll call you back as soon as I've talked with him."

Minutes passed. Finally the phone rang.

"Bad luck," the boys' father reported. "Torres checked out of his hotel and left no forwarding address."

"Can't we do something about finding him?" Frank asked. "Maybe he's going to contact Willie Wortman in New York City."

His father agreed that this was a possibility but said that he had to leave for Washington. He suggested that the boys fly to New York and see Wortman, and also check again with the bank's records regarding the curios. There might be a tie-in between the two men interested in the medallions. Perhaps they could pick up a clue on Torres and Wortman.

"What does Torres look like?" Frank asked.

"Short, slender, dark. He has a prominent chin and a black mustache."

"That description fits the blowgun man!" Frank exclaimed.

Mr. Hardy said that it could not be the same

man because Torres had been talking to him in New York at the time the missile had been fired at Joe.

An hour later Frank, Joe, and Tony were winging toward New York City on a double mission.

"First thing to do," Frank suggested, "is to call Wortman." As soon as they arrived in the city, they looked him up in the telephone book. His number was not listed and the boys went to see Mr. Cosgrove.

At the bank they were received cordially and given permission to investigate the shopkeeper's private records.

Finding nothing, the boys turned to a diary.

"Here's something of interest!" Joe exclaimed. "It says, first of all, that Roberto Prito did buy the medallions from Willie Wortman."

"That confirms part of Willie's story," Tony said.

"And according to the diary," Joe continued, "they were actually in the possession of Tony's uncle when he died. But now listen. In a separate notation it says, 'These medallions seem old and valuable. The strange design may indicate they are a clue to something. I will study them later.' "

"Mr. Cosgrove," Frank said abruptly, "may we look Mr. Prito's store over?"

"Of course. I'll get the key for you."

"Looking for Torres can wait," Joe said excitedly as the banker went off. "Let's try to find the medallions or the reason why they've disappeared!"

Twenty minutes later they were inserting the key into the padlock of the late Roberto Prito's shop on a Greenwich Village street.

"I'll lead the way," Tony said. "I know where the office is."

Bolting the door on the inside, the trio started for the rear of the empty shop.

Frank, a few paces behind, noticed an unusual showcase standing at an odd angle. His detecting instincts aroused, he moved the case and dropped to his knees. At first glance the floorboards under it looked the same as the others. But after close study Frank thought he could see the outline of what might be a trap door.

"Maybe there's a secret cellar under here!" he thought excitedly.

He tried to pull up the boards with his fingers. Failing, Frank pressed each board separately.

A moment later the whole section suddenly caved in. Frank lost his balance and crashed downward into inky blackness!

CHAPTER VI

Mr. Bones

PITCHING headlong into the dark cellar below, Frank struck his head sharply against a packing case. He fell onto the concrete floor, unconscious!

In the store above, Tony had led Joe into the small office at the rear of the long room. A high partition darkened this section of the shop. Tony switched on a light.

"Where's Frank?" he asked.

"He was right behind me—" Joe began, looking out the office door. "I wonder what happened."

"Frank!" Tony called. "Frank, where are you?"

They retraced their steps, and peered into the street. Frank was not in sight.

"It's just as if he were swallowed up in the—" Joe suddenly spotted the black rectangle behind the showcase.

"Look!" he cried. "A trap door! Frank must

have fallen through." He called his brother's name but there was no response.

From his coat pocket Joe took the small flashlight he always carried and beamed it below.

"There he is!" Joe gasped. "I've got to get down and help him! Must be a ladder here somewhere."

He beamed his light and found a short ladder hinged flat under the floor. Unhooking it, he let the ladder down. Both boys climbed into the cellar.

Joe carefully checked Frank's condition. "Wind's knocked out of him," he told Tony a moment later, "and he has a nasty bruise on his head, but I guess that's all."

As Joe spoke, Frank moved for the first time. He shook his head and made an attempt to sit up.

"Take it easy, fellow," Joe warned him.

With the boys' assistance Frank got to his feet. "What hit me?" he asked dazedly.

Tony raised the beam of his flashlight to the trap door and explained what had happened. Revived, but still somewhat groggy, Frank started for the ladder. "Guess I touched a secret spring."

"Just a second," Tony said. "Let's look in these packing cases. We may find something interesting."

Near him on the floor lay a claw hammer. Tony pried open a single board on each of the cases.

"Here's something I didn't see on the lists." He held up a small antique statuette of a Chinese horseman.

"Evidently Mr. Cosgrove doesn't know about these boxes," Joe remarked.

"Maybe the medallions are in here somewhere!" Tony said excitedly. "Let's have a look!"

But Joe noticed that Frank was not steady on his feet. "We'd better wait," he said. "Frank might have a concussion and should see a doctor."

"Okay," Tony agreed. "We'll do it tomorrow. Mr. Cosgrove might want to join us, too."

Joe examined the trap door and discovered how the hidden spring worked. Then he closed it and the boys departed.

It turned out that Frank had no serious injuries, but the doctor recommended a day's rest because of the nasty bump on his head. The trio registered at a hotel and after settling down in their room Tony phoned Mr. Cosgrove. He agreed to accompany the boys to the shop the next morning. The bank knew nothing about the curios in the cellar room, he said, and therefore they had not been listed.

Frank lay down on the bed, grumbling that he was really feeling fine.

"You'll feel even better tomorrow," Joe quipped. "Just stay put. Tony and I will do a little looking around for Torres while you relax."

At the information desk in the lobby Joe asked

"Wind's knocked out of him," Joe said

for the names of hotels in New York City where
Central Americans might stay to be with other
Spanish-speaking people, then he and Tony left.
First they tried Wortman's house, but he was not
home. Then they checked the hotels. It was sev-
eral hours later when they returned.

"Any luck?" Frank asked.

"No," Joe replied. "Torres has probably left
town."

After a hearty breakfast the next morning the
boys returned to the Prito shop. Mr. Cosgrove and
his assistant, Mr. Jones, arrived a short time later
and the examination of the secret cellar began.
They opened crate after crate.

"It appears that Mr. Prito stored his queerest
objects here," Mr. Cosgrove remarked, after
several cases had been unpacked and revealed an
array of skulls, animal teeth, an Egyptian toy
ferry, and all kinds of odd theatrical costumes.

"That's why I think there's a good chance of
our finding the medallions here," said Tony.
"The notation my uncle made proves that he
didn't consider them just routine curios."

Working methodically, the group had almost
completed the inventory by noon. But there was
no sign of the mysterious medallions.

"Wow!" Frank said as he opened the last crate,
a tall wooden box.

"What is it?" Joe asked.

Frank thrust one arm into the opening and

dragged out a human skeleton! Its white ghostliness at first shocked the group into silence. Then, as Joe realized it was a medical specimen, his humor came to the rescue. "A roommate for you, Tony." He grinned.

Frank lowered the skeleton to the floor. "Anybody who wants this bag of bones can have him!"

No one did. The executors inspected the skeleton and concluded from some penciled markings on the bones that it had been sold to Mr. Prito by some hard-up medical student.

"How about giving him to a medical school?" Mr. Cosgrove suggested. "He's a rattlin' good specimen."

"Good idea," Tony concurred.

Frank inspected the rest of the box. There was nothing in it. "I guess this concludes our search in New York for the medallions," he said in disappointment.

After making several calls to medical schools, Mr. Cosgrove said that a small private institution would be glad to accept the skeleton. He gave the boys directions, adding, "Tony, please leave the key to the shop at the bank when you're through. And I hope you find those medallions." The executor bade the boys good-by.

"Who wants to carry Mr. Bones to his next place of residence?" Tony asked.

Joe looked at his brother. "He can sit on your lap while we ride there. After all, you found him."

"Frank it is!" Tony laughed.

Grinning, Frank clutched the skeleton and climbed the ladder. The others followed him up and Joe stepped out onto the sidewalk to hail a taxi.

Presently one came along and Joe beckoned to the driver. The other boys with their strange companion were still out of sight in the shop entrance. Now they stepped outside. Tony padlocked the door and thrust the key into his pocket. The taxi pulled up to the curb.

"How many live passengers are you allowed to carry?" Joe asked the driver seriously. Then he saw Frank and Tony, the skeleton supported between them, starting for the cab.

"What's this—a joke!" The amused driver chuckled, and pretended to pull away.

"Wait!" Joe laughed. "Mr. Bones is harmless. We're taking him to Englander Hospital Medical School. Do you know where it is?"

"Sure." The man grinned. "Hop in. I'll drive carefully so we won't disturb your friend."

Placing Mr. Bones on the outside of the seat next to Frank, the group headed for the medical school. They had gone only a block when a police siren sounded behind them!

CHAPTER VII

A Street Chase

"THE motorcycle cop is after *us!*" Frank exclaimed. "He must have seen the skeleton!"

The sound of the siren grew louder and the taxi was ordered to pull over to the curb. The policeman, a big, red-faced man, climbed off his motorcycle and walked slowly back to the taxi. He stared at Mr. Bones.

"Where'd that come from?" he roared.

"We—we found him in the cellar," Tony explained, feeling a little foolish, "at Prito's Curio Shop."

"So!" the policeman exclaimed, looking stern. "That shop's locked up. I knew old Prito well."

Tony suddenly recalled that in his pocket was a letter from Mr. Cosgrove. "Just a minute, Officer. I can explain everything." The burly policeman read the letter, eyed Tony, then handed it back.

"So you're a Prito!" he exclaimed. "Now that I

got a good look at you, I can see you're like Roberto. Same snappy black eyes. Okay, boys, go ahead."

Twenty blocks north the taxi driver pulled into a side street and drew up to a white cement building.

Tony paid the fare and Frank picked up the skeleton. As the cab disappeared into the city's traffic, the boys walked through the hospital doorway. A young intern grinned as he passed them. "Who's your air-conditioned pal?" he gibed.

The boys chuckled and walked to a desk where a nurse was on duty. She directed them to the school, across a wide center court. There, a genial white-haired physician welcomed Mr. Bones and thanked the trio.

As they walked down the hospital steps, Tony said, "Should we try Wortman again before eating lunch?"

"Good idea," Frank said. "Also we must return the key from the shop to Mr. Cosgrove."

Wortman was still out. At the bank the boys were told that the newly found curios were being appraised at the shop and Tony could take whatever he wanted.

The boys went to the hotel, got their bags, and stuffed several of the smaller objects into them. Then they had a bite to eat, hailed a taxi, and set off to try Wortman's house for the third time. As their cab stopped at a busy intersection near the

East River, Frank suddenly gripped his brother's arm. "Look!" he cried. "Over there on the sidewalk. Willie Wortman!"

The recent visitor to the Hardy home appeared to be walking with another man. Wortman's broad shoulders partially blocked his companion from view. But as the taxi passed them, Frank and Joe caught a glimpse of the other man's face. He was dark-haired and black-mustached.

"Say, he could be the blowgun man or Torres! Stop here, driver!" Frank called, and the man pulled to the curb.

Frank paid him and the boys got out. "Tony, you stay here with the suitcases," Frank instructed. "Joe and I will talk to Willie."

"Okay," Tony agreed, and watched his pals dash after the two men.

The mustached stranger had now dropped slightly behind Wortman. As the boys hurried after them, the pair turned up a side street.

The Hardys dodged through the crowd. The red-haired sailor seemed to be enjoying his walk, whistling a tune. But the other man glanced from side to side uneasily. He acted almost as if he suspected someone were trailing him.

Willie Wortman suddenly looked back. Catching sight of the boys, he called out, "Frank and Joe Hardy!"

The mustached man also glanced back, then he broke into a run.

Frank stopped to speak to the sailor, and Joe chased after the stranger. But the man ran through an alley to another street and Joe lost the trail. Disappointed, he walked back to Frank and Wortman.

"What are you guys doing in the city?" the sailor was saying. He did not at all seem curious about where Joe had gone.

"Just came up for a short visit," Frank replied noncommittally. "We were on our way to the airport when we saw you."

"Have you found my medallions?" Wortman asked.

Frank shook his head. "Not yet."

"I'll be glad when I ship out," Wortman went on. "That curse business is getting under my skin. I've had nothing but bad luck lately." He scratched his head. "You know what? I think it might have been the cause of old Mr. Prito's death!"

"That's ridiculous," Frank told him. "And stop worrying about the curse. It's nothing but a superstition."

"I'll try," Wortman said, unconvinced.

The boys assured him that they would keep on searching for the medallions, then Joe said, "Sorry to have kept you from your friend."

"Friend?" Willie asked, puzzled.

The Hardys exchanged glances. If the suspect had been with him, why didn't Willie want to admit it? Or had the mustached man been following the seaman unknown to him? At that moment it seemed as if the latter possibility were true, so they did not pursue the subject. The boys said good-by and returned to Tony.

"Didn't learn a thing," Frank said. He flagged a taxi, and when they were settled inside, told Tony about their brief conversation with Wortman.

When they arrived at the airport, the boys were informed that they had just time to make the flight to Bayport.

It was late afternoon when the plane circled the Bayport field and landed. The boys drove back to town in the Hardys' convertible with Frank at the wheel.

When they reached Tony's house, Joe removed the curios from the Hardys' bags and helped his friend carry his luggage and the other articles to the front door.

"Phone us if you find anything developed while we were away," Joe said.

Tony nodded. "And I'll take these things to the museum right away."

Frank and Joe waited until·Tony had everything inside his house, then drove home. Mrs. Hardy greeted them at the door and said no telephone calls had come during their absence.

"It's been quiet and very lonely here with all my menfolk away," she said wistfully as Joe gave her a bear hug. "And please give Aunt Gertrude and me a little of your time. There are a lot of jobs around here that need my sons' attention."

For the next thirty-six hours the boys remained at home, cutting grass, weeding, and doing other chores. Tony called to tell them that everything had been quiet at the museum. Mr. Scath would be ready to confer with the boys soon.

At seven-thirty the morning of the second day after their return from New York, the boys were shaken out of a sound sleep by a frantic hammering at the front door.

"Who's there?" Joe called through the screened bedroom window.

A figure ran onto the lawn. It was Chet Morton. "Hurry out!" he cried.

Frank and Joe raced down the stairs and flung open the door.

"Look!" Chet said breathlessly, pointing.

On the floor of the porch a foot from the railing stood a six-inch-high, cone-shaped pile of ashes!

CHAPTER VIII

An Amazing Discovery

THE mysterious enemy's latest warning struck fear into Chet's heart. "This must be the work of that fire guy in the museum!" the chubby boy exclaimed. "And now he's—he's threatening you both personally."

"We've already been threatened personally," Frank replied. He told of the warning Tony had been given by Valez over the phone. "And this makes me think Valez was the person in the museum."

"Maybe he's putting a curse on you," Chet quavered. "The—the medallion curse!"

"Could be," Frank agreed, smiling. "But he may find it'll backfire."

Joe asked Chet what had brought him there so early. Chet explained that he was driving into town to buy a replacement part for one of the tractors on the Morton farm. "And I had an idea that I would be able to get some breakfast here if I left early!"

"Didn't you have any before you left?" Joe asked with a grin.

"Sure I did," Chet answered jovially, "but it was only a little one."

"Little one! I'll bet you polished off a dozen eggs!" Joe needled him.

As Joe and Chet watched, Frank got a small box and swept the ashes into it. "I'll get dressed and then take these to our lab and analyze them. You fellows may as well start eating. I smell blueberry muffins baking."

Joe and Chet went to the dining room. "Where's Frank?" Mrs. Hardy asked.

When Joe explained what his brother was doing, she sighed. "Oh dear! I'm afraid this enemy you've made is a dangerous one."

"Indeed he is," Aunt Gertrude stated crisply.

She would have gone on, but the boys' mother, sniffing, said, "Gertrude, I'm sure the muffins are done."

Chet was eating his sixth muffin by the time Frank returned. Dashing into the room he announced that the photomicrographs showed the burned material to be bones!

Chet almost choked on the muffin. "Maybe this is a warning that we'll all be roasted alive!"

"Take it easy, Chet." Frank grinned. "The bones were from a chicken."

"I wouldn't care if they were a pelican's," Aunt Gertrude said. "Your enemies must mean them as a final warning. Why don't you drop the case?"

"We can't back down now, Aunty. We must clear up the mystery."

"I suppose you're right," Miss Hardy conceded, and the boys' mother said she agreed.

After breakfast Chet went on his way to buy the tractor part. Joe phoned Tony to tell him about the latest warning and to find out if he had had any further word from Valez.

"Not a peep," Tony answered. "Do you think he's the one who left the ashes on your porch?"

"If he was," Frank replied, "it means he's still in Bayport. Want to come on a search for Valez?"

"You bet. Why don't you pick me up?"

The three boys spent the entire day sleuthing. After consulting the police records and learning nothing, they went to hotels, motels, and rooming houses. No one could help them.

"I sure hope we discover a lead soon," moaned Tony as they let him off at his house.

The Hardys drove home and put the car in the garage. When they entered the kitchen, Joe found a pinned-up note near the refrigerator telling them that Mrs. Hardy and her sister-in-law had gone out for dinner. The boys' supper was on the stove, ready for warming. Also, their father had phoned to say he was still in Washington but might be home later that night.

"Let's turn on the TV news before we eat," Frank said, and headed for the living room. As he led the way through the dining room, he stopped in his tracks. Then he pointed to the floor, crying, "Look at those buffet drawers!"

The four large drawers had been pulled out and their contents dumped out. Silverware and linen lay scattered on the floor.

"A burglary!" Joe exclaimed.

The boys dashed into the living room and the hall. These, too, were a shambles!

Frank and Joe ran through the house. From top to bottom every drawer in the place had been pulled out and rifled with one exception. The files in Mr. Hardy's second-floor study had not been broken into, probably because the intruder had not been able to force the lock.

"Joe," Frank said presently, "do you realize that nothing seems to be missing? Not silver, jewelry, or anything valuable. What *was* the housebreaker after?"

"Something he didn't find, that's sure."

Frank had just about concluded that the mysterious person was connected with one of their father's cases rather than their own when an idea suddenly occurred to him. He hurried back to their bedroom.

"I know what that fellow was after and he got it!" Frank called as he opened his closet door.

Joe dashed in. The cigarette-type box from

Tony's collection of curios was missing from the shelf!

"Maybe it wasn't so worthless after all," Frank reflected. He was about to add something else when he was interrupted by a car turning into the driveway.

"That's mother and Aunt Gertrude," Joe said. "Let's go down and tell them what happened."

The women were alarmed and shocked about the burglary, but after a quick check they confirmed that nothing had been stolen.

"Except for our curio box," said Joe.

"Oh that!" Aunt Gertrude said. "Perhaps it wasn't taken after all."

"What do you mean?" Frank was mystified.

"I borrowed it this afternoon to use for buttons I took off a suit. Let me see if it's still in my sewing machine."

Aunt Gertrude found the box. "I didn't think you'd mind," she said apologetically. "But I needed something—"

"Mind!" Frank exclaimed. "You might have done us a great favor, Aunty."

Miss Hardy looked blank. "Why? This isn't worth much, it's just a wooden box!"

"I'm not so sure. We'd better have a closer look at it. This box could have been the object of the man's search," Frank replied.

"What makes you think so?" Mrs. Hardy asked.

"It's the only souvenir from Tony's collection

that was in our possession," Frank explained. "The intruder at the museum might have seen Mr. Scath give it to me. If it is of value to him he might have come for it."

"Possibly," his mother agreed as Frank eyed the curio in his hand.

"You know," Joe said, "this looks like Central American mahogany to me. The same as the charred bits we analyzed."

Frank nodded. He examined the box carefully. Using pressure on each side, he tried to find out if it had a secret compartment.

"Here!" he exclaimed triumphantly a moment later. "It has a false bottom!"

With his thumbnail, Frank pried out a thin piece of wood built in above the bottom of the box. Wedged in it was a large, engraved golden coin!

"Wow!" Joe exclaimed. "Must be one of the medallions!"

"Now we know for sure the thief was after the box," Frank said. "Good thing Aunt Gertrude put it in her sewing machine!"

Mrs. Hardy studied the coin. "It looks like real gold," she said.

"And see!" Frank pointed. "It has the large opal Wortman spoke about!"

The stone was set on one of the lines crossing the medallion. "It doesn't look like a cheap stone to me," Frank added.

"Tony's uncle thought it had a special meaning," Joe said. "I have an idea that these engraved lines may form a map of some kind."

"What did Wortman say was on the other medallion?" Mrs. Hardy asked.

"A word," Frank replied. "Texichapi."

As Mrs. Hardy and Aunt Gertrude examined the gold coin, Joe said, "Perhaps these lines show the exact spot where a treasure is buried in a place called Texichapi. Remember what Torres told Dad."

"Let's look up Texichapi," Frank suggested and went for the atlas.

The boys studied the entire area from Mexico to the tip of South America. Their search yielded nothing. Nor was there any place in the world with that name.

"Apparently," Frank concluded, "Texichapi means something else. How about a secret password?"

Mrs. Hardy smiled. "It could be the name of a person. Some ancient king for instance, who was buried with a ransom in jewels."

Aunt Gertrude snorted. "Huh! Sounds to me like one of those peppery, fire-spitting South American recipes!" she exclaimed.

Everyone laughed and Frank said, "Probably the answer to the riddle depends on having both medallions. In the meanwhile, I think we ought to make a sketch of the exact position of these lines and where the opal is placed and also memorize it."

"Good idea," Joe said.

"While you're doing that," said Mrs. Hardy, "I'll warm up your supper."

The boys concentrated on the lines for several minutes, then tried drawing them on paper. It was necessary for both Frank and Joe to do this again and again until they had memorized the lines perfectly.

While the boys ate a late dinner, Mrs. Hardy remarked that she thought they ought to notify the police of the attempted burglary.

"I know as detectives you would like to solve this yourself, but as law-abiding citizens of Bayport we're duty bound to report it," she insisted.

"You're right," her sons agreed. Frank arose from the table and was about to call headquarters when the telephone rang.

"I'll take it," Aunt Gertrude called from the hall. A moment later she said, "It's Fenton! He's on his way home. Says he wants someone to meet him at the airport at nine o'clock."

"I'll go," the brothers chorused, then Frank said, "You pick him up, Joe. Drop me at the police station and I'll talk to Chief Collig personally."

"How about this medallion?" Joe asked. "Don't you think we ought to give it to Tony? After all, it belongs to him."

"You're right. Take it along and show Dad, then leave it at Tony's."

Joe put the medallion into his pocket and started for the garage. Frank followed directly and the boys set off on their errands.

"Whatever you do," Frank warned as he hopped out at police headquarters, "watch yourself."

Joe headed the car toward the airport. Halfway there he remembered that the highway was closed because of repairs. That meant he would have to take the lonely road that led past the museum.

The night was warm and the air still. "Like the night we brought Tony's stuff to the museum," Joe thought as the convertible purred along. He came to the building and slowed up. "Most of Tony's inheritance is in there now. But the most valuable piece may be the medallion I have," he mused, fingering the outline of the object in his sports shirt pocket.

As he drove along, there were fewer trees and the countryside became flatter. "About one more mile and I'll be at the field. It'll be great to see Dad and tell him firsthand all the new developments," Joe said to himself.

The road took a long bend to the right and then straightened out. As the car approached the highway, its headlights picked up a frightening sight. Several yards ahead a man lay at the edge of the road. Joe wondered if he was the victim of a hit-and-run driver.

The brakes screeched as he slowed his car. Near the prostrate figure, another person staggered forward, shielding his face from the glare of the headlights and signaled Joe to stop.

"What happened?" the Hardy boy asked as he jumped out to help.

"Don't know," the man mumbled in reply. Now Joe could dimly see his face—enough to learn that he wore a mustache.

Suddenly the roadside victim leaped to his feet. He too shielded his face so completely that Joe could see only his eyes.

Too late Joe realized that this was a trap. He tried to jump back into the car, but the man nearest him let go a powerful blow that sent him reeling against the left fender.

Recovering his balance, Joe lashed out at his assailant, but the next instant the other man struck him from behind. Quick as lightning, Joe whirled and connected with a smash that sent his adversary sprawling on the pavement.

If only a car would come by, there might be some hope for him. But none did.

"If I could get back behind the wheel, I'd have a chance to drive away!" Joe thought desperately.

He got one foot inside the car, but his assailants closed in again. They yanked him out and twisted his arms.

"Let go!" Joe cried out in pain.

He managed to tear away from their grip for a second, but one of the thugs shot a smashing blow to his chin. The boy blacked out!

When he came to seconds later he was gagged and a kerchief was tied over his eyes. He was bound hand and foot and lay in a thicket.

Joe realized that not once during the struggle had either of the men spoken a word. Even now, when a hand started to frisk him, not a sound came from his enemies.

To Joe's dismay, he felt the hand go into the pocket that held the medallion!

CHAPTER IX

The Peculiar Ping

LYING bound and gagged in the underbrush off the highway, Joe struggled to loosen the cords that cut into his wrists. Somewhere nearby in the darkness, his assailants were talking. They seemed to be very excited. Joe strained to hear what they were saying.

"They're speaking Spanish!" he thought, catching a phrase or two that he could understand. He heard one of them say, "Now we can find the place." A moment later the other broke out fiercely, "I want that fortune!"

The talk was suddenly drowned out by the sound of a car engine roaring to life. The men probably had concealed their car in the thicket along the road.

Joe wondered how they knew he would be passing this very spot. He concluded that they must have been eavesdropping at the open windows of the Hardy house when plans for going to the airport were made.

He heard his own car being driven off the road into the brush. Then came the sound of footsteps as the man returned. The driver of the getaway car stepped on the gas and sped off.

His motor made a strange pinging sound, which registered clearly in Joe's mind. "If only I could tail those men!" Joe said to himself.

At the airport, meanwhile, the plane from Washington had landed. Mr. Hardy, a tall, handsome man in his forties, looked around for a member of his family. Failing to see one, he went to the waiting room. No luck there. He inquired at the main desk if there was a message for him.

"Sorry, Mr. Hardy. We have no message for you," the clerk told him.

The detective shrugged. "I guess I'll just have to wait. Maybe there was a delay in traffic."

Ten minutes later Mr. Hardy decided to call home.

"I'm so glad you're back, Fenton," his wife said. "We've had a lot of excitement here, the kind we don't need!" She went on to tell him of the attempted burglary, but stopped herself short. "But you've already heard this from Joe," she concluded.

"Dear," Mr. Hardy said with a chuckle, "that's what I'm calling about. Joe's not here!"

"But he left in plenty of time to meet you," Mrs. Hardy said, worried.

Mr. Hardy tried to reassure his upset wife, saying that Joe might have had trouble with the car. Then he asked, "Is Frank there?"

Frank had just returned from his talk with Chief Collig. He came to the phone. "Hello, Dad."

"Do you know what route Joe was taking out here?" his father asked.

Frank told him of the detour, adding that Joe would have had to use the lonely road past the Howard Museum. "Dad, we found one of those medallions and Joe had it with him. Maybe he's been waylaid!"

"I don't like this. Take my car and start a search. I'll grab a taxi here and investigate from this end."

"Okay, Dad. I'll start right away."

Mr. Hardy collected his luggage and hurried from the building. Hailing a taxi, he briefly told the driver what had happened, then directed the man to the spot where he and Frank were to meet.

They set off along the highway over which there was now a heavy mist. Inch by inch they searched the roadsides with the taxi's spotlight, but there was no sign of Joe or the convertible.

"My son should be meeting us at any moment," Mr. Hardy said to the driver, "unless he found something."

At that moment the headlights of a car appeared from the direction of Bayport.

"This must be Frank. Blink your lights at him," Mr. Hardy said.

The taxi driver flicked his headlights several times and the approaching car answered the signal.

"Is that you, Dad?" Frank called as he pulled alongside.

"Yes. Any luck?"

"None. But I haven't examined the last hundred feet of roadside."

"Then we'll do that together," Mr. Hardy called out. "Turn around and move on slowly. We'll come directly behind you. Keep your eyes on the left side. I'll watch the right."

At a snail's pace, the cars headed out along the highway. Over fifty feet had been covered when suddenly Mr. Hardy saw the glint of a shiny surface in some high bushes.

"Stop!" he told the driver. As the taxi backed slowly, the spotlight picked up the glint again. Revealed in the glare was the windshield of the boys' convertible!

"Blow your horn!" Mr. Hardy directed. The taxi's powerful horn blasted several times. Hearing the signal, Frank returned to the cab in reverse.

He backed the sedan behind the taxi, leaped

out, and, with his father, thrashed through the brush. They quickly examined the convertible and the ground around it. There was no trace of Joe. But several sets of footprints were evident in the moist earth.

"Joe must have been ambushed," Mr. Hardy said angrily. "And they've either kidnapped him or left him nearby. We'll scour the whole area."

With flashlights, the two walked along both sides of the road, penetrating the clumps of underbrush. A few seconds later Frank discovered the trussed-up figure of his brother. Joe was still trying to fight free from his bonds and the gag, but his efforts were futile.

"Joe!" Frank cried out joyfully.

He removed the gag, and with his pocketknife severed the cords from Joe's wrists and ankles. Exhausted from his ordeal and his mouth as dry as paper, Joe could scarcely speak.

When they reached the taxi, the driver grinned. "I'm sure relieved that you're all right, boy. Whatever happened?" Realizing Joe could not talk, he reached under the seat and brought out a Thermos bottle of water.

The water revived Joe considerably and he gave a sketchy account of the holdup but did not mention the stolen coin. Mr. Hardy paid the taximan, included an extra amount for his time and trouble, and the man drove off.

"Now, Joe," Mr. Hardy said, "I'm sure that there's more to your story. Are you up to giving us the details?"

Joe nodded, saying he felt much stronger. He told about the ambush. "And now they have the medallion!" he moaned. "We've got to get it back for Tony! One of the men had a mustache. He might have been the blowgun man or Torres. There's just one other clue," Joe added, and explained about the ping in the enemies' motor.

"We'll notify the police at once," Mr. Hardy declared. "There's an outside chance we can pick up those thugs."

Frank and Joe hurried to the convertible as their father climbed into his sedan. Driving directly to headquarters, Mr. Hardy reported the incident. Chief Collig had the information teletyped throughout the state.

Then he assigned a patrolman to accompany the Hardys as they continued their search. The group, in Mr. Hardy's car, stationed itself at various main streets and incoming roads to listen for the engine with the strange sound. For an hour they patrolled the town without success.

Then at an intersection near the waterfront Joe heard the peculiar ping. "That's the car!" he cried out. "Let's get 'em, Dad!"

Mr. Hardy turned around and sped after the car, which was heading west now.

"He's going at a pretty good clip!" the officer

observed from the back seat. "You'd better open up and stop him!"

As Mr. Hardy closed the distance, the driver in the other vehicle sensed that he was being pursued. He instantly gunned his motor and for a moment the Hardys lost sight of his car. But Mr. Hardy maneuvered skillfully and soon caught up to the speeder.

"Pull over!" the police officer shouted as they passed him.

The driver realized that he had no chance of getting away. He slowed down and came to a halt at the side of the road. He was from out of town and confessed that he had stolen the car. Joe whispered that he was younger than either of the men who had held him up and did not speak with a Spanish accent.

As the police officer left the Hardys to drive his handcuffed prisoner to headquarters in the stolen car, the detective observed that they had helped the law, but as far as their own case was concerned, they would have to continue their search.

"But that ping," Joe reiterated. "I'm certain it was the identical sound. This guy was not driving at the time, somebody else was!"

Frank felt that his brother's observation should not be ignored.

"I think we ought to follow that car to headquarters and find out to whom it belongs," he declared.

"You're right," his father agreed. "We'd better check up on the owner." He drove back to headquarters.

The prisoner was just being booked when the Hardys arrived. Chief Collig waved to them as they entered.

"Thanks for helping us out," he said with his usual warm grin.

"Did you find out who owns the car?" Frank asked.

The chief nodded. "It's mighty popular—has been stolen twice tonight!"

CHAPTER X

A Shattered Window

"There goes our lead!" Joe exclaimed woefully when the Hardys learned that the car thief had picked up the automobile in a downtown street where it had obviously been deserted by the two men who originally had stolen it.

"But we'll keep a close lookout for your Spanish-speaking friends," Chief Collig assured Joe. "Let us know if you find out anything new, too!"

The Hardys promised they would, then went home. "We know two people who are after the medallions," Mr. Hardy mused. "Wortman and Torres. Possibly Valez, too. I suggest we get on the trail of Torres first."

"What about his patriotic society?" Frank asked. "Do you think that's on the level?"

Mr. Hardy shrugged. "It's possible. But since

he disappeared so mysteriously, it's also possible that he's after the treasure for his own benefit. Which would make him our archenemy number one."

"I wish we had something more concrete to go on," Joe mused.

"I know," Mr. Hardy said. "But right now we can only speculate. I have a hunch that Torres and Valez are working together."

"I wonder if Torres is the man who met Willie Wortman in the seaport and learned about Willie's medallions."

"Could be," Mr. Hardy agreed. "And Torres might have made up the fantastic story about the curse to frighten Wortman into giving him the coins."

"How do we start looking for Torres?" Joe asked.

"Before I turn in I'm going to phone a detective friend in New York City. Maybe he can work on tracking him down from that end. But I have a strong suspicion that he might be right here in Bayport!"

"Wow! What makes you think so?" Joe asked.

"If Torres and Valez are working together, Torres might have come here to see how Valez is doing."

While Mr. Hardy made the telephone call, the boys went upstairs to their bedroom. "It's good to have Dad back," Joe said as he turned off the light a few minutes later. Frank agreed heartily and fell asleep.

The next morning at breakfast a special-delivery letter arrived from Chicago for Frank. "It's from your friend Mr. Hopewell, who analyzed the missile for us, Dad," Frank said to his father.

"He writes that the South American Indians who make this unusual type arrowhead are known to be dead shots. Also, that this is the first of its kind he's seen in the United States."

"No wonder Mr. Scath couldn't identify it," Joe remarked.

The blowgun used to shoot such a missile, the letter explained, is considerably shorter than the usual seven-foot one.

Joe grimaced. "That's why I only got a glimpse of it," he remarked. "It must have been small enough so that the fellow could hide it under his shirt when he started running into the woods. Read on, Frank."

"These blowguns," Frank said, "are made by South American Indians of either a hollow reed or a length of ironwood bored through with a red-hot iron. Blowguns have crude sights, which are sometimes made of animal teeth. And the blowers often succeed in sending missiles with great accuracy up to distances of fifty to sixty yards."

"The man who fired at me certainly was a crack shot," Joe commented.

Aunt Gertrude, who had been silent up to this point, now burst out, telling her nephews once again that she thought they should drop the case as quickly as possible.

"Don't worry," Frank assured her, "we have Dad around to keep us out of trouble."

Fenton Hardy smiled at this remark, then said, "Even if they give up the case, likely these men would still keep after them."

The boys agreed and Frank added, "We're going over to Tony's now."

At the Prito home Tony was taking the morning mail from the box.

"Any news?" Joe asked him. "Any threats or missiles in your cereal this morning?"

Tony smiled, shaking his head. "Come on in," he said. "Glad you came over. I get pretty jittery around here wondering what's going to happen next."

"I'm afraid that our news is going to make you more jittery," Joe told him as they all went into the living room. He told Tony the details of the burglary, the ambush, and the loss of the medallion. "Terribly sorry I muffed everything, Tony."

"Oh, that's okay. I guess what's on the medallion is the important part. And you say you memorized it. No wonder Valez wanted me to—"

Tony stopped speaking abruptly. Something came crashing through the window!

"Look!" Frank cried, staring at an arrowhead

that had struck the wall and now lay on the rug. "It's exactly like the one that was fired at Joe!"

"And there's a note attached to this one, too!" Joe exclaimed. Frank picked up the object.

"I'd guess it was meant for Joe and me," Frank remarked. "The printing says, 'Stop your detective work!'"

Joe dashed out the front door. He was standing on the porch when the other boys came running out to search for the person with the blowgun.

"We're too late," Joe said. "He's gone!"

"Wait a minute," Frank said. "Judging from the angle at which the shot came in here, the man must have aimed from that lot diagonally across the street."

Near the wooded lot, a telephone lineman was at work on his truck. The boys hurried over to ask if he had seen anyone.

"Yes," the phone man replied, "I saw a man cutting through the lot."

"What did he look like?" Frank asked.

"Short. A skinny guy with a black mustache."

The boys nodded to one another. The assailant might have been Torres or the same man who had fired the first missile! And possibly he was one of the men who had waylaid Joe on the road to the airport.

"Do you suppose Dad's hunch about Torres being in Bayport is right and he's a blowgun man too?" Joe asked.

Something came crashing through the window!

"Could be," said Frank as Tony left to buy a new pane of glass.

Joe remarked to his brother, "As soon as we get this window fixed, we ought to comb the town from one end to the other."

"Right," Frank agreed.

Tony, with the help of the Hardys, soon had the new pane in place. Then they sat down to plan further strategy in tracking down the owner of the blowgun.

"Let's start our investigating at the bus terminal on the east side and have some lunch down there," Frank said.

"Good idea," Joe agreed, and Tony added, "Suits me fine."

The trio parked the car near the bus terminal, and had sandwiches in a nearby diner. Then the search began.

"Remember, we're to meet every half hour on the through street at the west end of the block we're searching," Frank reminded the others as they started off on their separate ways.

Three times the boys met, without any report of success. Then, heading north, toward the more thickly populated area of Bayport, Frank was startled to see a possible suspect approaching on the same side of the street. He was short, slender, and had a black mustache. When Frank got a better look at the man, he was fairly sure that he was the one who had shot the arrowhead at Joe.

But in the same instant the man had evidently recognized Frank. He whirled and disappeared down an apartment-house cellarway!

Frank dashed up the street after him. But just before reaching the apartment house he stopped. Had the man fled through the building? And was he armed? Suppose his enemy was aiming a deadly arrowhead at that very moment, ready to let it fly at him!

CHAPTER XI

A Near Capture

FRANK realized that he was exposed to the deadly aim of the blowgun marksman and quickly darted out of range, hiding behind a parked car. He ducked low to lessen the chance of being hit by his concealed enemy, and dashed across the street to take refuge in a doorway.

"Hey, Frank!" a familiar voice rang out as the young detective crouched, waiting for the mustached man's next move. "What are you doing—playing hide-and-seek?"

"Chet!" Frank cried as his stout friend ambled across the street toward him. "Hurry!"

"What's up?" Chet asked as he joined Frank in the shadow of the doorway. He told his friend that he was on his way to buy some horse feed.

Frank quickly related what had happened. Then he asked Chet to run to police headquarters two blocks distant. "Tell them to rush a patrol car to 48 Weller Street!"

Without even a backward glance, Chet hurried away. Frank kept his eyes glued to the building entrance but saw no sign of the fugitive. Minutes passed. Grimly Frank thought, "Did Chet get to the police safely?"

Then the welcome wail of a siren sounded as a radio car streaked around the corner. As it pulled up, Frank dashed from his hiding place.

"The man's in there!" he cried to Sergeant Murphy, who was in charge of four policemen. They leaped from the car. As everyone ran toward the house, Frank described the suspect. "And be careful," he warned. "He's got a deadly aim!"

"Cover the back entrance!" Murphy tersely commanded two of the officers. He instructed a third policeman to stay with Frank out front, then he and the fourth man dashed into the building.

The small crowd that had gathered to watch the action started to disperse when Sergeant Murphy and the other officer emerged from the building without a prisoner.

"Sorry, Frank," the sergeant said, "but we've found no trace of a black-mustached man. We checked every apartment. The superintendent tells me that no one in the building matches your description."

Murphy called back the other patrolmen. Frank, smarting with disappointment, thanked the police for their effort. The officers pulled away.

"I'm still not satisfied that blowgun guy is not in there," Frank told Chet. "Let's watch the place for a while."

They took up a position in a diner from which they had a clear view of the apartment house.

"Do you really believe he's still in there?" Chet asked, munching on his third jelly doughnut. "We've been here half an hour."

Without taking his eyes off the entrance, Frank replied, "If we wait long enough we may see him."

Ten more minutes passed. Frank began to think about his brother and Tony. They would be waiting at the crosstown avenue.

"Chet!" he suddenly gasped. "There he is now —what a break!" He pointed to a short, slender man leaving the front door of the building.

"But you said he had a mustache!" Chet exclaimed. "This man doesn't!"

"He must have shaved it off," Frank replied. "And he's wearing a different suit. But there's no question in my mind that he's our boy!" Quickly Frank opened the diner door and motioned for his friend to follow.

"What are we going to do?" Chet asked.

"Trail him!" Frank replied in a low voice.

Keeping a safe distance behind, the boys followed the man as he strode down the block. They stopped when he entered a hardware store.

"Listen, Chet," Frank said quickly. "He won't recognize you. Drift over to the store and see what's going on."

Frank ducked behind a large tree as his pal pretended to be looking at the display in the store window. Soon Chet hurried back excitedly.

"He's buying a window shade and some brackets!" he reported. "And I heard the clerk call him Mr. Valez."

"Watch it!" warned Frank, equally excited, as he saw Valez step outside the store. The man glanced in both directions, then started back toward the apartment house.

Frank asked Chet to return to the store and see what he could learn about Valez from the clerk. "I'm going to follow him!" he said, still keeping his eyes glued on the man.

"Where shall I meet you?" Chet asked.

"On the corner of the crosstown avenue," Frank replied. "Explain to Joe and Tony if you arrive before I do."

They parted and Frank hurried after the suspect. The man turned into the apartment-house entrance. He paused to open a mailbox, then disappeared into the foyer.

"He certainly seems to live here," thought Frank, wondering where the man had been when Sergeant Murphy had investigated the place. Then he headed toward the avenue to join his friends.

"We've been waiting half an hour and nothing to report," said Joe. "How about you?"

Tony and Joe listened wide-eyed to Frank's tale of discovering the suspect at the apartment house. His account was interrupted by the arrival of Chet.

"Your friend is the superintendent of the building," he said, "and has been for years. He's never had a mustache and the clerk told me he's well thought of in the neighborhood. His name is Eduardo Valez!"

"I still think there's a connection between him and the blowgun guy," Frank said. "He looks just like him. And Valez is the name of the fellow who threatened Tony. It can't all be coincidence!"

Joe nodded thoughtfully. "Perhaps Eduardo wears a fake mustache as a disguise, or"—and his eyes brightened—"he may have a mustached twin who's the real villain!"

"That's a possibility!" cried Tony. "The twin might have hidden in his brother's apartment while the police were searching the building."

"It's a far-fetched theory," Frank said. "But possible. Let's go home and talk this over with Dad."

"Sorry, fellows, but I promised to get back to the farm," Chet said.

Tony declared that he would like nothing better than to continue work on the case, but he was due to drive a truck for the Prito Construction Company the rest of the afternoon.

Frank and Joe went home and told Mr. Hardy of their latest adventure.

Immediately their father called his assistant Sam Radley and asked him to watch the building. When he had hung up, he said to the boys, "I'm going to check with the Immigration Service and see what I can find out about Valez. Meanwhile, I think you both should go and question him."

Eduardo Valez proved to be friendly when the boys told him they were detectives. His basement apartment was attractively furnished and on the mantel stood several carved figures.

"Are these wooden statues from your country?" Joe asked with interest. "They're beautiful!"

Without a moment's pause Valez replied, "Yes, they come from Guatemala. They're made of the best grade of mahogany," he added proudly.

Frank and Joe had the same thought. Some of the telltale ashes were of Central American mahogany. Had Valez left the burning embers?

Frank decided to pursue the subject of a brother indirectly. "Do you have relatives in Guatemala?" he asked casually.

"Ah, yes. Many. But I'm—how do you say?— hundred per cent American now," Valez replied in his soft Spanish accent.

"And relatives in this country?" Joe asked with

a disarming smile. "For instance, do you have a brother in the United States?"

The man's pleasant manner was ruffled for a moment. He dropped his eyes and his jaw tightened. Then he recovered his composure. Smiling, he said, "No. I have no brother in this country."

Further conversation led nowhere, and soon they thanked the man for his cooperation and left.

"What do you make of him?" Joe asked Frank on the way back home.

"He seemed on the level until we asked about his brother. I think we might be closer to the truth with our theory than we expected."

"Let's see if Dad found out anything worthwhile from Immigration," Joe said.

When the boys entered their home, Mr. Hardy called them into the living room. "Your man on Weller Street is a citizen," he reported. "He's been here more than five years."

"Does he have a brother in the United States?" Frank asked.

"No."

"I'll bet he does, and he's here illegally," Joe remarked.

"That's possible."

Just then Mrs. Hardy appeared and announced dinner.

When they had finished eating, the boys went into a huddle with their father on what angle of the mystery to tackle next.

"I believe we ought to wait for a report from Sam Radley," Mr. Hardy said. "Give yourselves a rest."

His sons took the advice and went to bed early. As they were dressing the next morning, Mrs. Hardy called to say that they were wanted on the phone. "It's Chet," she added.

Frank hurried to his mother's bedroom to answer on the extension. "F-Frank," Chet said in a quaking voice, "I just got a letter with a warning in it. Even has some ashes. The message says, 'You, too, are now cursed!'

"Frank," Chet groaned, "when I offered to help you fellows, I didn't bargain for anything like this!"

Frank said he was sorry and advised Chet to stay close to the Morton farm. "If you have to go to town, make sure you don't try it alone."

Just as Frank hung up, Joe was taking in the morning mail. A suspicious-looking envelope addressed to "Mr. F. Hardy and Sons" was among the letters. Quickly he slit the envelope, which was postmarked Bayport. It contained a quantity of ashes!

"Dad, come here quick! You too, Frank!"

When they reached the hallway, Joe read the printed note aloud: " 'We have sent warnings to your friends Tony Prito and Chet Morton. This is the last warning. Stop your sleuthing in this case or harm will come to you.' "

"No need to microtome these ashes," Frank said. "Central American mahogany again!" He held up one unburned bit of the familiar wood.

Meanwhile, at the Morton farm, Chet's pretty, dark-haired sister Iola was worried about him. She had never seen him more nervous. And she too was upset over the note. Hoping to take her brother's mind off the threat, she proposed a steak roast that evening at Elkin Amusement Park.

"We'll go early and have some fun on the rides before we eat."

Iola, who was usually Joe's date, soon extracted promises from Callie Shaw, the attractive blonde who often dated Frank, and two other girls, Maria Santos and Judy Rankin, to come along. Then she invited Tony and the Hardys.

"Swell idea!" agreed Joe, who answered the phone. "We haven't seen you girls for a long time."

"We've reserved fireplace Number Twelve for our picnic," Iola explained. "An attendant will watch our food and lay the fire for us."

"Great," Joe said. "I'd like to do nothing for a change."

"Oh, you'll have to do the barbecuing," Iola replied. "And of course we'll go on the rides and visit the House of Horrors!"

"Fine! We'll pick up the other girls shortly after five," Joe replied.

"Meet us at the farm," Iola said. "We've fixed up something special. 'By now!"

About three o'clock Frank phoned Callie to tell her the plan. "Frank, a funny thing happened here a short while ago. I didn't think anything about it at the time, but now it worries me."

"What is it?"

Callie said she felt that unwittingly she had told a stranger about the picnic plans. A man had come to the Shaws' selling novel kitchen gadgets.

"I bought a couple of them," Callie went on. "Then suddenly the man said, 'You're a friend of Frank Hardy's, aren't you? Nice guy.' "

"I hope you agreed," Frank said teasingly.

Callie did not laugh. "I'm worried, Frank. He seemed so nice, but now I realize he asked me a lot of questions. He may be a spy—one of those men from the patriotic society Iola was telling me about."

Frank asked if the man spoke with a Spanish accent and had a mustache.

"No," Callie said. "He was tall and blond, about thirty."

"Well, stop worrying," said Frank. "Just concentrate on having a good time."

Callie promised to do so, then Frank put down the phone. Despite his lighthearted attitude about the incident, he was alarmed. There was no question in his mind that the kitchen-gadget salesman was a phony.

"But if he has any evil intentions, we'll be safer at the amusement park—with so many people around—than at any other place," Frank reasoned.

After picking up the three girls and Tony Prito in their father's car, the Hardys set off for the Morton farm at five o'clock. When they arrived, the group learned that Chet had piled hay into his father's truck, so they could all go on an old-fashioned hayride to the amusement park.

"Len is going to drive us," Iola announced.

A big cheer went up from the boys. Len Wharton, a good-natured former cowboy, had recently come to work at the Morton place.

Len grinned. "Shucks, I figured that if I was seventeen I sure wouldn't want to be stuck with the drivin'."

Zigzagging through the back-country roads, Len stretched the trip to Elkin Park into an hour-long ride. As the picnickers got out, he said, "You just call me at the farm when you want to get on back."

The baskets of food were carried to the reserved fireplace, where the attendant stored them away.

For an hour the four couples whirled about on the thrill rides, and laughed their way through the House of Horrors.

"And now—the best for last," Iola announced.

"Before we go back to the fireplace, let's take a ride on the roller coaster."

The young people boarded the bright red cars and strapped themselves in.

They reached the summit and rolled smoothly around the bend. Suddenly they snapped into the steep dive! Maria and Judy screamed as the cars streaked past the white uprights. Hitting the bottom of the run, they plunged into the blackness of a short tunnel, and emerged on a level center track that passed the ticket booth. As the coaster began another climb, Frank uttered a gasp.

"Joe!" he exclaimed to his brother in the seat behind. "He's here! Near the ticket booth!"

"Who?" Callie asked.

Not wanting to worry her, Frank merely said it was a man for whom he and Joe were looking. Through the rest of the breathtaking swoops and turns the Hardys could think of little else. The chances of spotting the blowgun suspect again in the crowd milling around the park were small, nevertheless they would try.

The instant the ride was over, Frank and Joe excused themselves and darted in and out of the crowd, but did not find the man.

"I'm sure that he has left the park," said Frank. "But this means he's still in Bayport. So our case isn't so hopeless after all."

When the boys reached fireplace Number Twelve, they found the picnic baskets placed on a redwood table. The attendant had laid the fire of kindling and charcoal. It was ready to light.

Chet knelt at the fireplace and set the fire. The flames, fanned by the stiff breeze, licked rapidly through the kindling. In a short time a fine blaze was roaring.

"When it dies down, we'll put on the steaks," Chet announced.

Suddenly there came a terrific explosion from the fireplace! Chet fell backward several feet from the flames as glowing embers rained down on the entire group.

CHAPTER XII

The Black Sheep

"HELP!" Iola cried frantically. "My hair's on fire!" Desperately she beat her palms against her head, screaming in terror.

Frank ripped off his jacket and flung it about her head, snuffing out the flame that endangered the frightened girl. Leading her away from the roaring fireplace, he said reassuringly, "You're okay now."

Iola, though still shaky, managed a laugh. "It's one way of getting a new hairstyle."

Chet declared he was all right—aside from having the breath knocked out of him by his fall. The scare over, they all tried to figure out what had caused the blast. Had some explosive substance been sprayed on the kindling? Or had someone planted a crude bomb in the fireplace?

"In any case," thought Frank, "the salesman at Callie's *was* a spy!"

The girl ran to his side. "I told you! I'm the cause of this!" She quickly repeated her story of the salesman to the others.

"Did you mention fireplace Number Twelve to the man?" Frank asked.

"Yes, I did. Oh dear!"

Frank put a hand on her shoulder. "Callie, no real harm has been done, so forget it," he said soothingly.

A crowd quickly gathered and began to ask questions. The gray-haired attendant, who had been making another fire, hurried over.

"I didn't put anything but wood and paper in the fireplace," he said nervously.

"Was anyone near this spot while we were gone?" Joe asked him quietly.

The attendant said a man with a mustache had offered to help him lay the fire in Number Twelve. "I told him I'd do it myself," the man continued. "He did hang around, though."

The Hardys did not voice aloud the suspicion that the salesman had told Torres or Valez the picnic plans. They merely assured the attendant that he was not to blame. The girls found another fireplace, and Chet and Tony carried the baskets over to it.

"Joe," said Frank, "we'd better search the embers in Number Twelve. We might find a clue."

"Right."

After sprinkling a can of water over the still-burning wood, they raked through the damp remains for evidence.

"Guess this is it," Frank said. He pulled out a small metal container. "A homemade bomb."

"This character, whoever he is, isn't fooling around," Joe said grimly.

"That's for sure," said Frank and reached into the ashes. He took out a window-shade bracket. "Take a look at this."

"Must have been part of the device that triggered the bomb!" Joe said. "Say, didn't Chet tell us that our friendly superintendent bought some brackets at the hardware store?"

"Right," Frank replied. "Valez is definitely mixed up in this!"

The boys decided that they would say nothing to their friends about the find, but the next morning would investigate Eduardo Valez again. Try as they might, the group found little pleasure in the meal. The shock of the explosion and the narrow escape of Chet and Iola from serious injury had caused them all to lose their appetites.

"Even I don't feel hungry," Chet lamented. "We should have eaten on the way out here."

Iola phoned Len to come and get them.

"At least," Frank said, smiling, "we had fun here before the explosion."

Early the following day Mr. Hardy and his sons drove across town to question Eduardo Valez.

"Good morning," the superintendent said

affably as the boys introduced their father. "Come right in."

"Mr. Valez, you'd better tell us the truth this time!" the detective said as they entered the apartment.

"Wh-what do you mean?" the man replied.

The detective told in detail the happenings at the amusement park. As he unfolded the account of the explosion and the narrow escape of the young people, Valez's face whitened.

"I—I am not the man you are searching for," he said slowly. Looking at Joe and Frank, he said, "I am sorry I did not tell you the truth at first. Now I will explain."

"Thank you," Mr. Hardy said. "Go ahead."

"The man with the black mustache," Mr. Valez continued with a pained expression, "is my brother. He is the—what you call—black sheep of our family. Six of us children and he is the only one to break the law."

"What is his name?" Mr. Hardy asked.

"Luis."

"Where is he now?" Frank asked.

"I do not know, but he was staying with me for a short time."

"Which explains the mustache mystery," Joe remarked to Frank.

"Luis sneaked into this country," Valez went on. "He promised me the day before yesterday he would return to Guatemala at once, so I did not turn him over to the authorities when they came here asking about a mustached man. Luis left here while I was on an errand at the hardware store."

"Buying brackets," Joe murmured.

"Did you say something about brackets?" Valez asked quickly.

"Yes. We found a bracket in the remains of the fire," Joe replied.

"That is what I went to the hardware store to get," Mr. Valez added. "There was a bracket missing from one of my apartments. So I had to buy another. And I got a new shade while I was there. Luis must have taken the old bracket."

The superintendent went on to tell Mr. Hardy and the boys that he was astonished to learn that his brother had become a suspect in a case of violence. "I thought Luis had come to the United States to get away from some little trouble at home. He said it blew over, so he was going back. Always I have defended my brother," said Eduardo, clenching his fists, "but now I see I can no longer do this."

"Is there anything else you think we should know?" Mr. Hardy asked.

"Maybe this is not important," Valez replied, "but a couple of small mahogany objects disappeared too. Luis might have them with him."

The Hardys quizzed the superintendent about the possibility of a connection between mahogany and any Guatemalan superstitions. Valez explained that among certain people in Central America there was one such superstition, adding, "It's said if a person sends the ashes of a piece of native mahogany to his enemy, that man will be rendered powerless to harm the sender!"

Frank frowned. "That's a very strange idea."

Valez could give the Hardys no further information, so the detective and his sons thanked the superintendent and left. On the sidewalk, Frank and Joe speculated on the mysterious piles of warning embers and ashes.

"Luis must have burned some of his brother's mahogany pieces," Frank stated.

"But why the chicken bones?" asked Joe. "Unless," he added thoughtfully, "he didn't have any of Eduardo's wood pieces handy at the time. He probably figured we wouldn't know the difference."

Around the corner, where Mr. Hardy had parked his car, the trio met Sam Radley. The assistant reported that the mustached man had not been back to the apartment while either he or his relief man was on duty.

When the Hardys returned home Aunt Gertrude told the boys that Tony Prito had called. He had told her that Mr. Scath had estimated the collection to be worth about two thousand dollars and had asked him to take away the things he wanted.

"You're supposed to go over there with Tony this evening," Aunt Gertrude concluded.

Shortly after dinner Frank and Joe drove off in the convertible to Tony's. There, they transferred to Mr. Prito's small pickup truck.

"Let's get Chet," Joe said. "I'll bet he's just sitting around worrying about the threat he received. Maybe he'd enjoy helping us."

The others grinned and Tony said, "You know how he loves to work—not at all!"

Chet was finally persuaded to join the group and they drove off. The museum had closed for the evening by the time the boys arrived. Mr. Scath suggested that the four boys go to the storage shed at the rear of the museum grounds for some crates and pack the articles in them.

Tony donated some pieces to the museum which the curator had selected, then said, "We'll carry the rest of the stuff back to my place. Let's put it in the cellar."

As the boys went to the rear door, Mr. Scath handed the key to Chet, who was the last one out. The four crossed the dark yard and entered the shed. A stack of various-sized crates was piled near the door.

"Now I know why you asked me to come along," Chet said. "You needed a strong man like me."

"That's right." Frank laughed. "So we'll give you the privilege of carrying two crates instead of one at a time."

"Okay." Chet grinned. "I'll take two little ones."

Suddenly Joe put his finger to his lips. "Sh-h!" he warned.

The boys stopped short. A faint cry had sounded from the museum.

"Help!"

It was Mr. Scath's voice.

"Help!" The cry died out.

CHAPTER XIII

News of Buried Treasure

DROPPING the crates, the boys ran to answer Mr. Scath's call for help. After the two outcries, they had heard nothing more.

"I don't see how anyone could have broken in," Frank said.

"I'm afraid it's my fault," Chet admitted as they reached the rear entrance. "I didn't lock this door. Thought we'd be right back."

"Someone must have sneaked in here the moment we left," Joe groaned. "I hope Mr. Scath hasn't been struck by a shot from the blowgun!"

Frank turned the knob and they hurried inside. Chet locked the door.

"Be careful of a sniper!" Frank warned the others. "And keep together!"

The curator was not in sight and when Frank called he did not answer.

"He must be on the side of the building nearest the shed," Joe suggested. "His voice wouldn't have carried from the other sections."

He led the way into the Egyptian Room and switched on the lights. Mr. Scath was sprawled on the floor, unconscious! The boys rushed over.

"There's blood on his face!" Tony exclaimed. "He's been hit in the head!"

"And look at his pockets!" Frank cried. "They've been pulled inside out. Joe, you and Tony search the building for the assailant, while Chet and I attend to Mr. Scath."

Joe and Tony headed for the opposite end of the museum. Frank and Chet knelt beside the injured man and inspected the head wound. Fortunately it was not deep and the curator's color was returning to normal. A moment later Mr. Scath gave a low moan and his eyes flickered open.

"Help me up," he said feebly, trying to rise.

"Lie still," Frank urged. "Don't try to move."

He recalled having seen a first-aid kit in the curator's office and asked Chet to get it.

The stout youth hurried off. A whiff of spirits of ammonia revived Mr. Scath. Frank gently swabbed away the blood. Luckily the man had been struck only a glancing blow.

"Feeling better?" he asked.

"My head feels clearer," Mr. Scath replied. He sat up with Chet's assistance.

"Here, let me put a patch over that cut," Frank said.

When this was done, the boys helped the curator to his feet and back to his office.

"What happened?" Frank asked, after Mr. Scath had seated himself in a comfortable chair.

"I was in here alone, waiting for you fellows, when I heard a noise in the Egyptian Room. I went to investigate."

"Did you see someone?" Chet asked.

"Yes. There was a masked man standing alongside the first big column. He demanded that I hand over the Texichapi medallion from Tony's collection."

"Yes?" Frank said eagerly as the man paused.

"I told him that I had no idea what he was talking about," Mr. Scath continued. "Then he pulled out a blackjack and threatened me. I got a bit flustered—tried to fight him off—and I shouted a couple of times, hoping you'd hear me. Then he struck me and I blacked out!"

"What was his build?" Frank asked.

"Short, thin. Had black hair."

Frank whistled. "The blowgun man or Torres! We'd better phone the police."

"If it was Luis Valez," Chet exclaimed, "he didn't go back to Guatemala after all!"

Frank nodded, then called Chief Collig and told him about the attack.

"We'll be right there!" the chief responded.

Meanwhile, Joe and Tony had searched the entire north section of the museum without finding the curator's attacker. The skylight had been checked but found to be locked on the inside. The boys went back to join the others.

Not finding them there, they decided that Chet and Frank must have led Mr. Scath back to his office. As they were about to check there, Joe suddenly noticed something on the floor. He picked it up. "Tony!" he exclaimed. "This is a new Guatemalan coin!"

"Do you think the guy who slugged Mr. Scath dropped it?"

"That's my guess. Let's check your curios," Joe suggested. "If the intruder was Valez, that's what he was after."

They went through a gallery containing old musical instruments and jewelry. As the ceiling light was turned on, the boys gasped. The glass had been neatly removed from one of the cases. Every ring, bracelet, and necklace was gone!

At that moment a siren sounded at the front entrance and the night bell rang insistently.

Joe and Tony hurried to the museum office as Chief Collig strode in with two other officers. Frank, who had let them in, followed. Quickly they were told about the accident and theft, and started a thorough search of the building. But it was soon ascertained that the attacker had escaped.

Chief Collig said, "From now on we'll keep

a guard around the place on a twenty-four-hour basis. Sampson, you stay here right now. I'll send out a teletype on the missing jewels and a description of the intruder."

Mr. Scath handed a spare key to Sampson, then said to the boys, "Come back another time and pick up the curios." Everyone but the officer on duty left.

The next morning Frank and Joe decided to question Eduardo Valez again, hoping he might have heard from his brother.

"No, I have not heard from him since you were here with your father," the man replied.

"Did Luis ever tell you the exact nature of the trouble he had in his country?" Frank asked.

"No," the superintendent replied. "He did say something about an argument over a buried treasure, but Luis is such a braggart I paid little attention."

"Buried treasure!" Frank exclaimed. "Did he ever say anything about medallions?"

"Medallions?" Eduardo Valez mused. "No, he never did. Oh, I am so sad about the whole affair."

The boys left, feeling sorry for him. As they passed the next apartment house, they saw Sam Radley standing guard. They gave no sign of recognition. Neither did the detective.

"I think we ought to spend the rest of this day making an intensive search of Tony's curios for that Texichapi medallion," Joe proposed. "That's what Luis was hunting for when Mr. Scath discovered him, so maybe we've overlooked some hiding place where Tony's uncle put it."

"We'll get Tony and Chet," Frank answered.

At two o'clock they all met at the museum. Mr. Scath, still wearing a bandage on his forehead, smiled as the boys started off to the shed for the crates. "I hope we have better luck today!" he said.

They brought the crates to the basement and went to work. As each curio was examined closely, those to be taken by Tony were placed in a crate. The others were returned to the shelves. An hour passed. One crate had already been filled, but they had not found the medallion.

Chet Morton, still upset over leaving the museum door unlocked the night before, had worked hard, trying to make amends.

At the moment Chet was fingering a solid mahogany, highly polished ball. He picked it up and removed a foil wrapping that covered part of the surface. His sharp eyes detected a thin, almost invisible line that went completely around the circumference of the ball. In his excitement to get a closer view of it, the ball slipped out of his grasp. It hit the cement and rolled across the floor.

"Playing games?" Joe teased.

"I'm sorry," Chet groaned, going after the ball. "I wasn't playing. I—"

He broke off as he stooped to pick up the ball.
It had started to come apart at the seam. A strip
of rich blue velvet showed in the opening. Then
he saw the brilliant glint of metal!

Prying apart the two sections, he cried out,
"Fellows, come here quick! I've found the second
medallion!"

Gleaming in the light, on its velvet bed, lay
the coin. It was the size of a half dollar. Carefully
Frank lifted it and held it for the others to see.

"It's one of the medallions Wortman was talking about!" Frank said. "See the word Texichapi?"

"And there are strange engraved lines similar
to the ones on the stolen medallion," Joe added.

Frank slipped the coin back into the ball. "I'd
like to show this to Dad and examine it very
carefully," he said.

"Okay with me," Tony answered. "But after
what happened to Joe with the first medallion,
watch your step."

The crates were taken to the Prito house; then
Frank and Joe went home to talk to their father.
To ensure complete privacy from eavesdroppers,
the trio went to the laboratory. There they examined the ball and the medallion. They concluded that the ball had been designed originally
as a secret place to hold small pieces of valuable
jewelry.

The boys drew from memory the pattern of

lines on the stolen coin, then traced the new ones. They concluded that the lines from the two coins, when superimposed, seemed to indicate a map.

"It must show the area near the treasure that Luis Valez is looking for," Frank remarked.

"And the opal probably marks the place where the treasure is hidden," Joe added. "Boy, I'd like to find that spot myself!"

"But it's in Texichapi—the land of nowhere," Frank reminded him.

"Let's hope we can learn what country Texichapi is in," said Mr. Hardy. "Meanwhile, you boys had better memorize the lines on this medallion and then we'll place it in my safe."

This was done. Then the boys and their father sat down in his study and continued to discuss the mystery.

"I wonder," mused Mr. Hardy, "whether your friend Willie knew the value of both medallions. This one feels like solid gold to me and it certainly has the same luster as a gold piece. Maybe Willie was just acting dumb because he feared Tony might refuse to sell him the coins once they were located."

"That's quite possible," Frank said.

"I know that you've consulted all kinds of maps to locate a place called Texichapi," Mr. Hardy continued, "but I'm going to make another try to find out where it is."

"It's one of the medallions Wortman was talking about!" Frank said

Being personally acquainted with various Central and South American consuls, the detective telephoned them one by one and inquired about the name. None of the men had ever heard of it.

Later in the evening Mrs. Hardy had an idea. "Fenton," she said, "why don't you phone my friend Mrs. Putnam? Her husband Roy has just come back from an expedition."

"The Central American explorer?" Mr. Hardy asked. "Why, that's a great idea. But it's much too late to call anyone now."

"Not Roy Putnam," Mrs. Hardy said. "He stays up half the night reading. I'll get him for you."

Mr. Putnam answered promptly and Mrs. Hardy turned the phone over to her husband. The explorer became so interested in a brief account of the mystery that he offered to drive over at once.

"I'll be there in about twenty minutes," he promised.

The family went into the living room to await him. A thunderstorm came up shortly, and Mrs. Hardy closed all the windows in the house except the one near where they were seated. The wind whipped up sharply, banging a shutter on the east side of the house. Frank went to fasten it.

Soon the doorbell rang. Joe opened the door. The explorer, a man of commanding figure, took off his raincoat and shook hands with everyone.

"It's about time we got together," he said with a smile. "My wife speaks often about you."

"But you're so rarely at home," Mrs. Hardy replied.

"That's right." Mr. Putnam smiled. "I've just returned from Guatemala, in fact."

"I'm sure then," Mr. Hardy said, "that you can give us a lot of help. Did you ever hear of Texichapi?"

A bolt of lightning flashed, startling them all. Then Mr. Putnam said, "When you mentioned Texichapi a moment ago, I was surprised. I never dreamed that anyone way up here would have any knowledge of that place!"

"Where is it?" Frank questioned eagerly.

"Well, first of all," Mr. Putnam began, "have you ever visited Guatemala?"

The Hardys said they had not.

"As you know," Mr. Putnam began, "the country stretches from the Pacific to the Atlantic, just below Mexico. It's a rugged land—full of canyons, towering mountain ranges, and volcanoes.

"It's mostly Indian in population, and has some wonderful ruins. Even out in the deepest jungle, in the most unsuspected places, one finds buried temples and palaces."

A crash of thunder made it difficult to hear the explorer for a moment. Then he continued:

"Guatemala has beautiful cities. Colors splashed everywhere—bright red roofs, light-blue and white-walled houses, tropical flowers—parks full of them."

"Now how about Texichapi?" Mr. Hardy asked mildly.

"Oh, yes." Mr. Putnam smiled a bit sheepishly. "Texichapi," the explorer began, "is a name given by a small tribe of Indians, the Kulkuls, to a mysterious and perhaps even mythical area many miles from Guatemala City. I've heard various rumors about the region."

"What are some of them?" Frank asked.

"The main one concerns a great treasure buried there," the explorer went on, and the boys jumped in amazement. "Though I have many times tried to find out more about Texichapi, the Indians are very closemouthed. It's not inconceivable that the Kulkul tribe guards the secret to Texichapi."

"Boy, would I like to find it!" Joe said eagerly.

Aunt Gertrude spoke up for the first time and snapped, "Why, those Indians might kill you if they caught you looking for their treasure!"

Mr. Putnam smiled tolerantly. "The Indians in Guatemala respect the white man. No, you're more likely to have trouble with an occasional band of hostile, renegade Ladinos who have fled to the mountain regions.

"Ladinos," the explorer explained, "are Spanish-speaking, mixed-breed people. They are very proud and do no manual work like laboring in the fields or carrying loads. Mainly, they own stores and cantinas and hold political offices."

Mr. Hardy nodded thoughtfully, then said, "Mr. Putnam, do you know whether any Guatemalans have a secret society that was organized to uncover this treasure or any other in the interest of their government?"

"Yes," Mr. Putnam replied. "The only trouble is I don't know just which society you mean. They come and go—pop up all of a sudden, make a big noise, and disappear as quickly."

The explorer went on to say that he had heard of no such group lately but he could find out. "If you'll allow me to use your phone," he said, "I'll check with a friend in Guatemala City whose business it is to investigate such groups."

"Please do so," Mr. Hardy said, showing the visitor to the hall phone.

"They won't mind my calling at this time of night." Mr. Putnam grinned good-naturedly. "It's three hours earlier there."

The Hardys returned to the living room while Mr. Putnam put through his call. Several minutes passed before the man came back.

"My friend Soldo, who works for a government agency, tells me that there are rumors of another so-called patriotic society forming right now," Mr. Putnam reported as he sat down. "His agency would welcome any information about it. If something subversive is going on, he says, there'd be a good chance of nipping the plans in the bud."

The Hardys noticed that Mr. Putnam had suddenly slumped in his chair, giving a tremendous yawn. Almost at the same moment, Frank and Joe began to experience a queer lethargy.

Their father, too, felt himself growing drowsy. With a great effort, he tried to speak, but at the same time both his sons and Mr. Putnam slipped from their chairs to the floor, unconscious.

Fighting to remain awake, the detective got to his feet and moved across the room to assist his sleeping wife and sister. But before he could reach them, he stumbled and blacked out!

CHAPTER XIV

Confessions

As the storm raged, the Hardy family and their guest remained in a deep stupor on the living-room floor. For twenty minutes none of the silent forms moved. Then the wind shifted, and the rain started pelting through the open window into the room.

Frank, lying nearest the window, was within its range. The continual spray across his upturned face gradually aroused him. Fighting desperately against the drowsiness that still engulfed him, the boy struggled to get up. He looked dazedly around.

"They're all asleep!" he thought. He wondered what had happened to cause this weird scene. Suddenly an answer came to Frank.

"Sleeping gas," he decided. "Where did it come from, though?"

He went to close the window against the storm. As he did so, he noticed the screening had been cut. On the floor below the window lay a large strip of screening and several punctured, greenish pellets the size of a golf ball.

As he picked one up and examined it, Frank mused, "These are gas pellets and must have been tossed in here."

He decided that the noise of the storm and the family's rapt interest in Mr. Putnam's story would have prevented their noticing any sound at the window.

The rest of the family and Mr. Putnam began to revive. Frank, sensing that the danger of any lasting effect had passed, turned his thoughts in another direction. Who had hurled the pellets? Suddenly he remembered the screening on the floor. Maybe their enemy climbed into the house! He could have cut a small slit first, thrown the pellets, then cut out the large piece to get through.

As if in answer to his unspoken query, Frank saw a masked man coming down the stairs! The intruder, apparently startled by Frank's unexpectedly quick recovery, jumped over the remaining steps and dashed for the front door.

Frank made a flying leap. Before the man could turn the doorknob, Frank crashed into him, sending him sprawling on the hall floor.

Catlike, the masked man leaped to his feet. A blow caught the boy on the cheekbone and split the skin. Enraged, Frank hurled himself at his adversary and knocked him against the steps!

While the fight was going on, Joe stood up unsteadily and glanced around. Out of the corner of his eye he saw the struggle and staggered to the hall. He was just in time to see Frank leap back as the man rolled off the stairs.

Frank, momentarily dazed by the impact of his tackle, raised both fists as his adversary scrambled to his feet and pulled a blackjack from his pocket.

"No, you don't!" Joe roared. He leaped forward and swung a left uppercut to the man's chin that sent him to the floor.

Both boys jumped the intruder, stripped him of his blackjack, and pulled off his mask. The blow-gun suspect!

"You're Luis Valez!" Frank accused him.

"You have made a big mistake," the suspect replied.

Holding the man in a tight grip, the boys searched him quickly. Frank located a gas pellet in one of their prisoner's jacket pockets. In another, Joe felt something smooth and hard. He pulled it out. The Texichapi medallion!

"How did you get into the safe?" Frank asked in a steely voice.

The man admitted hacking it with a hachet which he had left upstairs. Then he refused to answer any more questions.

Frank, recalling that gas sometimes made a

victim talk, decided to use a ruse to make Valez confess! Pretending to tear open the end of the pellet he had found, he said in a firm voice:

"This will make you talk!"

The ruse worked. "Don't do that!" the man cried, terrified. "I will tell everything!"

By now, the others in the living room had recovered from their enforced sleep. They were amazed that the boys had caught the burglar.

Frank said to the man, "Now tell your story."

"You are right," the stranger began slowly. "I am Luis Valez from Guatemala. But please do not arrest my brother Eduardo. He knows nothing of what I do."

"And what *are* you doing?" Mr. Hardy asked.

"I cannot tell you. All I want is to be shipped home to Guatemala."

"How can you go back without this medallion?" Joe asked, holding it up. "You wouldn't be very popular if you returned empty-handed."

The man hung his head and Frank demanded to know who had sent him to steal the coin. The dejected Guatemalan admitted that it was Torres, head of a patriotic society of which he was a member.

"We are searching for the treasure of Texichapi," he said quietly. "That is why we wanted this coin."

"And that's why you stole the matching medallion," Joe said.

Valez denied this.

"How do we know you're not just part of a gang that's planning to keep this treasure and not give it to your country?" Mr. Hardy asked. "You've got a great deal of explaining to do. The police will want to hear it."

Frank went to the telephone and called headquarters. "We didn't have to go chasing the blowgun man this time," he told the lieutenant on duty. "Caught him right in our house. He's the one who fired at Joe."

As Frank hung up, Valez protested vigorously that he had never seen Joe before tonight. In spite of the Hardys' accusations, the man stuck to his story. He admitted trying to buy Tony's curios, but denied having sent any threats or knowing anything about the stolen scimitar, the ashes, the museum theft, or the explosion in the picnic fireplace. He became sullen and seated himself on the steps, staring at the floor. But the Hardys knew he was lying.

Mr. Putnam, who until this moment had been looking on, got up and approached Frank and Joe. "Good work, boys!" the explorer praised them. "By the way, my friend in Guatemala will be glad to help you at any time. And now I think I'd better get home."

The Hardy family thanked him for coming and for the information he had given them.

"Just call me if you need anything," Mr. Putnam said as he started for the door. Then he smiled. "But next time ask your other guests to leave their sleeping gas at home."

When Mr. Hardy returned from escorting Mr. Putnam to his car, he said, "It's too bad Willie Wortman isn't here too. He probably could give us some valuable information about Valez." The detective winked at his sons.

At the sound of the sailor's name, the prisoner leaped to his feet. "Willie Wortman!" he exclaimed. "What do you know about him?"

"Plenty," Joe said noncommittally.

"How did you meet him?"

"Willie paid us a visit," Frank replied, "and told us about the medallions."

The Guatemalan's face went white with fear.

"Valez, what do *you* know about Wortman?" Mr. Hardy asked.

The prisoner admitted having met Wortman in a Guatemalan seaport. "That sailor!" Valez snorted in disgust. "I fix him! He talk too much!"

When Valez had cooled down a little, Frank asked him where Wortman was at the moment.

"I don't know," Valez replied. "I have not seen him for a long time."

The Hardys decided that there was little use in trying to question the man further.

"Here come the police!" Joe said as a car pulled to a stop in the Hardy driveway.

Before leading Valez away, Chief Collig informed the Hardys that the stolen museum jewelry, including the scimitar, had been located in various pawnshops around the state. All of the proprietors described the seller as a dark-haired and mustached man who spoke with a Spanish accent. He had given his name as Romano.

Still protesting that he was innocent, Valez was handcuffed and led through the downpour by two officers to the waiting car.

The next morning a surprise awaited Frank and Joe when they joined their father at the breakfast table.

"Boys," he said, "I'll stake you to a trip to Guatemala—that is, if you want to go."

"Wow! Do we!" Joe exclaimed and Frank beamed.

The detective said he felt that they had come to an impasse in solving the mystery from the Bayport end. Furthermore, if an unscrupulous group was after the ancient treasure, the Guatemalan government would no doubt appreciate having it located by honest people.

"So we have two assignments," Frank said. "To find the treasure, and to keep it from being stolen."

Mr. Hardy nodded. "I'd like nothing better than to go with you, but since I'm on an important government case, I can't leave the country. I would like you to have someone with you, though. How about Tony and Chet?"

"Let's find out," Frank urged, and went to the phone.

Both Tony and Chet were flabbergasted to hear about all that had transpired at the Hardy home in the space of a few hours. The idea of a trip intrigued them, and Mr. Prito and Mr. Morton gave permission for their sons to go.

The boys booked a flight for ten o'clock the following morning. It would land them at one New York airport from which they would go to another field for the journey to Guatemala.

As the Hardys each packed a suitcase and a duffel bag, their father recommended that they again test their memories on the markings on the two Texichapi medallions. Both had them letter-perfect.

"I think Tony and Chet should also learn them," Frank said, and phoned the boys to come over.

"Let me tell you a trick," Mr. Hardy said. "You begin, Chet. Take a good look at our drawings and then, with your eyes closed, sketch them in your mind. Mark Twain did this to memorize the Mississippi River when he was a cub river pilot."

Soon both boys had memorized the strange lines which the Hardys believed were directions to the treasure.

At eight o'clock Mr. Hardy left. He wished the boys luck on their exciting trip, reminding them to get in touch with Mr. Putnam's friend at the consulate if they needed help.

"Sam Radley will drive you to the airport and keep his eyes open for suspicious persons."

When Sam appeared the next morning he reported that Luis Valez had refused a lawyer and admitted nothing.

"He may change his mind," Frank remarked.

As he and Joe kissed Mrs. Hardy and Aunt Gertrude good-by, both women came close to shedding tears. "Please take good care of yourselves," their mother pleaded, and their aunt said, "Watch out in those mountains, you could catch your death of cold!"

Sam Radley, in high spirits, cheered up the women with his jokes, then he and the brothers drove off to pick up Tony and Chet. At the airfield, while the boys were waiting for their bags to be weighed, a familiar voice said, "Hello, there!"

Willie Wortman! The big redhead seemed as jovial as ever. "I missed you by a few minutes at your house," he said. "I was up this way and dropped by to see how you were making out with those medallions. I'd sure like to get 'em back."

The four boys looked inquiringly at one another. Did he or did he not know anything?

Feeling that secrecy was the best policy, Frank said, "Willie, we've had no luck so far."

"That's a shame," Wortman said. "Don't forget the curse that's on them. I expect bad luck to overtake me any time."

The Hardys felt sure that Willie's trip to Bayport had something to do with the man who was now in jail. Watching the seaman closely, Frank said, "Your friend Luis Valez was arrested last night."

"Valez arrested!" Wortman cried out. "What for?" Then the sailor suddenly realized what he had said. His eyes opening wide, he asked, "How did you find out I know Valez? Did he tell you?"

"No." Joe grinned. "We just guessed it."

Wortman took no offense at this. "You *are* good detectives," he said.

Joe went on, "Valez is the fellow who told you about the medallions' curse, isn't he?"

Paling slightly, Wortman nodded. Joe now questioned him about the man with him on the New York street. Willie denied having been with anyone.

Frank looked straight at him. "Do you know a friend of Valez's who sells kitchen gadgets?"

"No."

Just then an announcement came over the loudspeaker that it was time for passengers to board the New York flight.

"Come on," Tony urged.

Frank hung back a moment. "Willie," he said, "that salesman was responsible for us boys and some girls nearly being seriously injured. That's one of the reasons Luis Valez is now in jail. You'd better watch the company you keep!"

The boys moved off, leaving Wortman with his jaw sagging and his eyes popping.

When they reached the gate, Sam Radley was waiting for them. In a loud voice he called, "Have a swell trip, fellows!"

The detective took hold of Frank's arm and pulled him aside. In a quick whisper he said, "Frank, I found out there's a Ladino man on the plane masquerading as a woman. I've got a hunch that it has to do with your case. Watch out!"

CHAPTER XV

Volcano!

AMAZED by Sam Radley's warning about the masquerader on the plane, Frank hurried after the others.

"What did Radley tell you?" Joe asked as the quartet started up the ramp steps to the cabin.

"Let you know later," Frank said in a low voice.

The boys gave their boarding cards to the attractive stewardess, then took their seats.

The giant plane taxied out along the runway and swung into position for the take-off. The signal came from the tower and within seconds they were in the air headed toward New York.

As the craft flew out over Barmet Bay, Frank, pretending to be trying for a better view of the harbor, leaned close to his brother. "Sam thinks there's a Ladino man dressed as a woman on the plane," he whispered tensely. "I guess he got a good look at her through his magnifying spectacles and figures she has a shaven face and is wearing a wig. He thinks this 'woman' may be mixed up in our case."

"Good night!" Joe exclaimed under his breath. "But say, what gave Sam the clue to his Ladino stuff?"

"Don't know. That's what I mean to find out."

Sitting back in his seat, Frank joked with Tony. He got up, leaned over his friend's shoulder, and in between laughs told him the news.

"Pass it on to Chet," he whispered. Then he started to look through a magazine.

"Do you think this person is trailing us?" Joe asked softly. "I thought with Valez in jail we were safe."

"There's a whole patriotic society, remember?" Frank remarked.

A little while later he stood up, saying he was going to look for the Ladino. Halfway down the aisle he spotted someone he suspected. A woman seated alone!

She had very dark skin and black eyes, and wore a dark-blue dress with a small white collar. Her hair was black with a Spanish-type comb in it. A narrow shawl was pulled around her bony shoulders. She was reading a book.

"That's a man wearing a wig, all right," Frank thought as he reached the stewardess and asked to see the passenger list.

The Spanish-looking woman was listed as Mrs. John Macky, New York City.

As Frank walked toward his seat he saw that the so-called Mrs. Macky was turning the pages of her book. Her hands were large and masculine.

A moment later he said to Joe, "Radley was right. And I have a hunch the fellow in disguise may be Torres minus his mustache. He has a prominent chin, as Dad said."

Joe was thunderstruck. "Do you think Willie was here to see him off?"

"Who knows?" Frank replied. "Anyway, Radley will keep an eye on Willie."

The problem of what strategy to pursue raced through the Hardys' minds. Was the suspect really Torres, and did he know that the boys were headed for Texichapi? If so, they must try to elude him and in turn follow him.

At Frank's suggestion he and Tony exchanged places and the Hardys' friends were told of the plans.

"Wait until we arrive in New York before we take any action," Frank said. "Then we'll use an FBI tactic. Let the enemy follow us till he tips his hand."

When the plane reached the airport, the boys succeeded in being the first to descend the steps to the runway. Mrs. Macky, they noted, was not far behind. As Frank had planned, the quartet walked shoulder to shoulder to the baggage counter to await their luggage.

Suddenly the boys stopped dead in their tracks.

"Tony Prito!" a loud voice was calling. "Telegram for Tony Prito!"

Seeing the youth hold up his hand, a messenger hurried over, handed him an envelope, and left.

"Who could be sending me a telegram?" Tony mused. "My folks?"

Opening the envelope, he pulled out the message. It was not a telegram at all, but a hand-printed warning: *Stay out of Guatemala or your life will be in danger!*

"And the thing's full of ashes!" Chet whispered.

"Where's the fellow who gave it to us?" Joe asked. "We'll find out where this came from!"

But he had disappeared.

"This settles it," Frank said grimly. "We get out of here as fast as we can." He looked around for "Mrs. Macky," but the masquerader was not in sight. "Come on, fellows!"

By this time their luggage had come through and the boys quickly claimed it. Frank whispered directions and they followed him to a limousine that would take passengers into the heart of the city. In the line of those waiting stood Mrs. Macky!

"We're in luck!" Joe thought elatedly.

The Bayport group waited until the suspect was seated in the limousine and other people piling in. Then they made a dash for a waiting taxi and rode off.

"Good work, Frank," Joe said.

"Where to?" the driver asked.

Frank directed him to the international airport where they would board the plane that was to fly them to Guatemala. When they reached the mammoth, busy airport, Tony began looking around frantically.

"What's up?" Joe asked.

"The number of bags," Tony replied. "We had eight. And now I can count only seven!"

Tony was right. One bag was missing!

"And it's mine!" Tony moaned. "It had all my clothes in it."

"Couldn't we go back and get it?" Chet asked. But Frank pointed out that they could never make it in time to catch the Central American flight.

"What'll I do?" Tony asked woefully.

"You'll just have to dress like an Indian!" Joe laughed.

"That might be a smart thing to do," Frank said. "In Indian dress, with his black hair and dark skin, Tony might pass for a native guide."

"Sure," Tony agreed. "I might be able to learn things the rest of you couldn't that would help us in our search. Only trouble is"—he sighed—"I can't speak any Spanish or Indian dialect."

Frank grinned and Joe said, "Oh, you can act like an antisocial type and say nothing."

The boys boarded the plane. Presently a stewardess came around with magazines and Tony asked whether she had any literature on Guatemala. The pleasant young woman brought him a book in which he was soon absorbed.

As the plane took off and the other boys stared out the windows at the ground below, Tony discovered an item of interest in the Guatemalan book. It concerned an eccentric type of Indian, who rarely spoke and roamed the countryside looking for the sacred quetzal bird. "This would make a perfect disguise for me," thought Tony. In another chapter, he studied and memorized some simple, useful words common to all Indians.

Then, excited by the prospect of playing the role of a native, he showed the book to his friends. Tony flipped to a page where a picture of the quetzal bird was shown. About the size of a turtle-dove, it was emerald green in color, with a shining crown containing ruby-red and blue tints.

"Listen to this! The bird cannot live in captivity, and is loved by the people for its free, wild, independent spirit. Because of this, the rare quetzal bird has become the national symbol of Guatemala."

The jetliner winged its way down the coast and the four boys finally dozed. They slept through the night. At sunup they were over the Caribbean, nearing the eastern coast of Guatemala.

"There's the shoreline!" Joe cried. The boys noticed that the vivid blue sea water was changing to a lighter hue and caught a glimpse of the white strip of beach and the mountains beyond.

At the Guatemala City airport, the boys were cleared through customs. They collected their bags, then went outside to look for a taxi. A driver approached and introduced himself as Jorge Almeida.

Smiling broadly as he picked up two bags, Almeida said, "This way, *amigos*. I have a fine taxi waiting for you!"

Grinning, they followed his slender but wiry figure to an old car parked by the curb. The driver put their bags in the trunk and the boys got inside.

"Better take us to a hotel first—some place where they have good food," Frank directed.

"Hokay!" Jorge Almeida replied.

As he drove, the man chatted amiably and answered the boys' questions. He told them he knew of no place near Guatemala City named Texichapi. "But," he admitted modestly, "I have not been everywhere."

Jorge pointed out the sights of the plaza, and drove them around the big square and past the arcades where natives sold food from small booths.

In the center of the plaza, men were arranging chairs on a bandstand in preparation for the evening's concert, Jorge informed his passengers. Gaily dressed pedestrians were strolling along the promenades, admiring the beds of gorgeous, bright-colored flowers.

"Look at those men!" Joe exclaimed.

A group of small-statured Indians in red serapes, shawl-like blankets thrown over their shoulders, sat crouched in the shade of the arcades. "Tony, that's what you'll look like in your new clothes!"

Tony grunted. *"Si,* me search for quetzal bird!"

The others grinned at his odd combination of Spanish and American-Indian dialect.

"Everybody like that bird." Jorge laughed as he circled the square and finally stopped at the entrance of a clean, whitewashed hotel near the end of the plaza. "This place hokay!" he announced, unloading the baggage.

Frank added a generous tip to the taxi fare and Jorge said, "You fine boys! I drive you cheap from now on."

The boys thanked Jorge for his offer, obtained his address, and promised to get in touch with him when they were ready for another ride.

After checking into the hotel and stowing their gear in two airy bedrooms, they set out to learn what they could about the road to Texichapi.

"Look!" Chet exclaimed, pointing out a booth near the square where native dishes were displayed. "I'm going to get some *tortillas.*"

The others agreed to wait for him. They sat down on a park bench as Chet walked over to the booth. Nearby, two men were playing marimbas and singing in low-pitched voices. Joe, Frank, and Tony were enjoying the music when a few minutes later Chet came running toward them, crying, "I'm on fire! Get me water!"

He was fanning his tongue with his hand and the others realized that he had probably eaten a red-hot chili pepper. Tony pointed to a small drinking fountain nearby and said, "Use that!"

Chet dashed to the fountain and stuck his head into the spray. Grimacing with the burning sensation in his mouth, he then opened it wide, keeping his face under the jetting arcs of water.

"He probably thought he was eating a tomato," said Joe.

Their friend finally left the fountain and walked toward them. Looking at the boys accusingly, Chet said, "I saw you all laughing but it was no joke."

As he mopped his dripping wet hair with a handkerchief, the others apologized.

"We'll test the food first after this," said Joe. "Don't forget that down here they like it highly spiced."

The boys then continued walking around the promenade. At the side opposite the hotel, Joe spotted a shop that sold Indian goods. "Let's go in and find a traveling outfit for Tony," he suggested.

While Tony was buying wool trousers, a warm jacket, and a *sute* to wrap around his head, the others admired serapes, moccasins, and embroidered shirts. Finally Tony's costume, including a shoulder-length wig, was wrapped and the group returned to the hotel.

Half an hour later the quartet appeared on the plaza. Tony made an odd-looking companion in his Indian clothes and wig.

"Now, I'm ready for the quetzal bird!" he said, laughing.

A Ladino, standing nearby, stared darkly at Tony and spat on the ground. Then he savagely spoke a Spanish phrase that Frank understood to mean:

"A curse on you!"

As the boys hurried away, Chet said fearfully, "You might get us all in trouble, Tony, pretending to be hunting for their sacred bird."

"I won't mention it again," Tony promised. "In fact," he smirked, "me silent, serious Indian. Your guide."

After eating lunch in a nearby restaurant Jorge had recommended, the boys hunted up Mr. Putnam's friend. To their disappointment, he had gone to Brazil.

"We'll just have to inquire where Texichapi is," said Frank.

But when they did, the various men shook their heads. No one had ever heard of it. A few knew where the Kulkuls lived—in a northwesterly direction from the city, but were vague as to any details about them.

"I guess that we'll have to map out a route to

the Kulkul area and take a chance that the Indians will tell us where Texichapi is," Frank concluded.

He bought a map and the boys pored over it until late that night. A route was finally decided upon.

"We can go one hundred miles to this point in a car," Joe pointed out. "After that, we'll have to hire mules."

"We'd better let Dad know how we're making out," suggested Frank, and sent an airmail letter.

The next morning the hotel clerk directed them to a food supply store. Here they purchased a quantity of canned goods and bread. In the course of their conversation with the shopkeeper, he remarked that he had a relative at the one-hundred-mile point who rented mules, saddles, and blankets to tourists who wanted to explore the mountainous country.

They went to Jorge's house to make arrangements for him to drive them. His face became one expansive smile when he was given the assignment. As the boys walked back to the hotel, Joe remarked, "Doesn't it seem queer to you that we haven't been followed or bothered by our enemies?"

"How about the one who cursed Tony?" Chet asked.

"I don't think he was part of any gang," Joe replied. "He probably was one of those people who are superstitious about the quetzal bird and thought Tony was making fun of it."

"Don't forget," said Frank, "that we don't know who all our enemies are. We may meet more of them yet. I suggest that we leave here early tomorrow morning before anyone's up."

By phone they completed arrangements with Jorge, and soon after sunrise he was at the hotel entrance. The clothing the boys were not taking was checked at the hotel, and they set off in rough, warm mountain apparel. Tony, in his Indian costume, stowed the two duffel bags in the taxi.

"You turn Indian?" Jorge grinned. "Almost fool me," he added.

"Good," said Tony. "But I don't know how to manage this blanket!" He grabbed his serape as it started to slip off his shoulders. Jorge explained how Tony should secure it. Then the boys climbed into the car and started their exciting journey to look for the Texichapi treasure.

In high spirits, Jorge sang a witty native tune as the road began to climb into the mountainous country. "Now we make with the speed!" he announced, driving like a daredevil around a sharp turn.

The boys' hair was standing on end as the car screeched around another narrow bend, where the valley dropped away a thousand feet below.

"What's the matter?" Jorge asked.

"Please take it easy!" Chet moaned. His friends also thought this would be a good idea.

"Hokay," Almeida replied. "Soon the road— she gets more steep and like a snake."

Just then a great roaring sound rumbled through the mountains. "What's that?" Tony cried out.

"Volcano, I think," Jorge replied, concern on his face. "We see."

As the car completed the next sharp turn, the boys gasped. The mountaintop above them was exploding in a giant fountain of liquid fire! The boiling 2000-degree lava was already pouring down the slope. In a few minutes it would reach the road!

"We're trapped!" cried Chet.

"No, no, we have ten minutes," said Jorge. "We beat it!"

He raced the car along the road, but had gone only a hundred yards when there was another ominous rumble. Then, almost directly in front of the boys, a stream of lava came down.

"We're lost!" cried Tony, as the lava spray came within a few feet of the car.

"I get out!" Jorge cried. "Beat other fire river before it run across road."

He turned the taxi back along the treacherous roadway. Sweat poured down his face as he steered the swaying car.

"We'll never make it!" Chet groaned.

CHAPTER XVI

A Kidnapped Companion

Jorge Almeida worked desperately to bring his taxi past the danger area. It swayed and skidded. But Jorge did not slow down as he headed for the serpentlike turn.

"Faster! Faster!" urged Chet, eyeing the hundred-foot-wide, red-hot lava flow above them.

It was so close that the boys could feel the intense heat from it.

With another burst of speed the taxi shot around the turn. Too late the boys saw that the road was blocked by several massive rocks that had rolled down the mountainside.

"We'll crack up!" Tony yelled.

Jorge braked the car and succeeded in slowing it. But not enough. The taxi smashed into the boulders, throwing the boys violently forward.

All were dazed, but managed to climb out of the car. Jorge, who was stunned, was pulled out by

Joe and Frank. The trio scrambled over the boulders, following Tony and Chet in their desperate flight to get as far away as possible from the path of the lava. Seconds later, the destructive stream gushed over Jorge's wrecked car, carrying the taxi with it to the valley below.

"Whew!" sighed Joe, when they stopped running and looked back at the fiery spectacle. "Boy, that was a close call!"

"Thank goodness we're all safe!" said Frank.

"All but my little taxi," said Jorge. Then suddenly his face brightened. "It's hokay! We got insurance. I will get new taxi from the company," he said, "with louder horn."

"But what'll *we* do?" asked Chet. "We've lost our supplies and equipment. All that food," he moaned.

"We get more!" Jorge said cheerfully.

But the boys did not share his lightheartedness. They were miles from any city or town and now had no means of transportation.

"My cousin Alvero Montero owns *finca*," Jorge said. "It is long distance but we can walk it easily. He has mules we can borrow."

The boys gladly accepted the offer and followed Jorge down the mountainside. For the remainder of the day, they trekked through the thick undergrowth of the valley.

Shortly before dusk, the group arrived at the charming Montero plantation. Work had ended for the day, and as the boys approached, the aroma of cooking reached them.

A tall, pleasant-looking man, dressed in work clothes, appeared at the front of the main house.

"My cousin," said Jorge, and hooted a signal to his relative.

Montero waved and hurried to meet his unexpected guests. "Welcome, Jorge!" he cried in Spanish. "You bring friends? Good. You are all just in time to take dinner with us."

Then, as the group came closer, he noticed their disheveled condition. "You have been in a battle with rebels?" he continued. "And what are you doing on foot? Where is your taxi, Jorge?"

Almeida introduced the boys and told his cousin of the near tragedy. After expressing his sympathy, the planter looked in amusement at Tony's disguise. "You had me fooled." Montero laughed. "And I see Indians every day. They work here."

He invited the group inside and presented the boys to his beautiful Spanish wife and their two small sons. Their host provided the visitors with swimming trunks, and they swam in the cold, clear mountain water of a dammed-up stream near the house. Later, they sat down to eat a lavish steak dinner.

The hungry boys had never tasted a better meal, especially the dessert—bowls piled high with papayas and pineapples.

After dinner Señor Mr. Montero, smoking a slender black cigar, told them that he had not heard of Texichapi. But he would be glad to lend them four mules to take them to the point where they planned to rent animals and equipment for the rest of their trip.

"If anyone in Guatemala knows about Texichapi," Montero continued, "it will be a remarkable old Indian who lives in a village across the next mountain."

"Will he talk to us?" Frank asked.

"Yes," Montero replied. "His name is Tecum-Uman. Tell him I sent you—he knows me well."

Jorge arranged with his cousin to let the travelers stay overnight and they all slept soundly. Early in the morning he excused himself, saying he would go back to Guatemala City on one of Alvero's mules and report the loss of his car to the taxi company.

The Hardys and their friends prepared to start for the village where Tecum-Uman lived. Señor Montero gave them a supply of food and handed each boy a machete. "With this, you can chop your way through the thickets."

After thanking the planter for all the favors he had shown them and saying good-by to his family, the boys mounted their animals. Señor Montero said that the mules could be left at the place where they would pick up the others. Two of his workers would bring them back later.

With Tony still wearing the Indian outfit, the quartet began their arduous ride. Because the road was blocked off, they were forced to take a path through the dense forest of the valley.

"I wish we had a guide with us," Chet remarked.

"What do we need a guide for," Joe asked, "when we have Big Chief Tony? He will lead us to Tecum-Uman."

"*Si*, we no get lost, *amigos*," Tony said with a stony face. "Only trouble is, wig itches!" He scratched his head and laughed.

The talk shifted to the treasure.

"What do you think it is?" Chet asked.

Frank said, "I've read that when Cortez's captain, Alvarado, conquered this country over four hundred years ago, he reported that the Indians had great quantities of gold and precious jewels. Some of this treasure was buried by earthquakes, floods, and volcanic eruptions, and people have been searching for it ever since."

"Don't get your hopes too high," said Joe. "You may end up with some worthless three-eyed stone monsters."

Several times along the way the quartet overtook small groups of homeless refugees whose houses and land had been devastated by the same volcano which nearly cost the boys their lives. The elderly people and children were riding burros, but the middle-aged group trudged along on foot, carrying their salvaged goods on the three-foot-high *cacaxtles* strapped to their heads and shoulders with cowhide thongs.

Each time the boys met these groups, Tony tried out his dialect, asking the people about the location of Texichapi. To his delight, they understood him and seemed to accept him as a member of some other tribe, but the boys were disappointed not to learn anything about Texichapi.

Traveling at a brisker pace than the heavily laden people, they quickly moved out ahead of the refugees. In midafternoon, as they approached the Indian village where Jorge's cousin thought Tecum-Uman might live, the four riders came upon another group of natives on the narrow trail. Tony prepared to try out his disguise once again.

As the group rode up, the mounted Indians suddenly spotted Tony and cried frantically, *"Shaman! Shaman!"*

They made a quick flanking movement and encircled the stunned boys. Before Tony could even open his mouth, the attackers had grabbed him, pulled him onto a horse ridden by the fiercest-looking of the lot, and galloped off.

"They've kidnapped him!" Chet cried out.

CHAPTER XVII

The Weird Ceremony

As Chet made a mad dash after Tony's kid-nappers, Frank called him back.

To his amazement, the Hardys were grinning.

"How can you stand there laughing when Tony's in trouble? Why don't we *do* something?"

"Calm down, Chet," Joe said. "Didn't you hear what those Indians were yelling?"

"It sounded like *shaman*," Chet replied.

"Exactly," Frank said. "And that means sooth-sayer." Shading his eyes from the sun, Frank peered ahead. "Looks as if they're taking Tony to the village. They probably think he's some sort of traveling magic man."

Chet sighed in relief.

Joe, however, was worried. "I sure hope Tony can get away with it," he reflected. "If they find out he's not a shaman—"

"Suppose we all wander into the village," Frank

proposed. "By the time we get there they'll probably have elected Tony chief of the tribe!"

With Joe leading Tony's mule, the procession started along the trail.

"What's so wonderful about a shaman?" Chet questioned.

"He's a mixture of priest and poet," Frank replied. "Whatever the shaman says goes. He is supposed to be able to see into the future. One ritual he performs is called 'telling the mixes.' "

"What's that?" Chet asked eagerly.

"When a person plans to do something on a certain day," Frank explained, "and he wants to be sure it's the right time, he calls on a shaman. This man arranges some red beans from a pita tree and then he burns some stuff called copal, says his mumbo jumbo, and announces to the man whether it's the lucky day or not."

"We could use a shaman for our Bayport High football schedule," Joe remarked with a laugh.

Suddenly the trail turned sharply into the cobbled main street of the village. Adobe shacks with thatched roofs lined both sides. Indians huddled against the poles that supported the shop roofs.

There was no sign of their friend or of the group that had borne him off. But Frank felt certain that the Indians would release Tony as soon as they discovered their mistake.

"While we're waiting, let's ask one of these men about Tecum-Uman," he suggested.

Frank went along the line asking the same question of each of the stolid, poker-faced natives. He got only a cold stare in return.

"Well, that went over like a lead balloon," he said a bit angrily. "Let's look around for Tony."

At the end of the street stood a low whitewashed building with a long porch. It looked like a shop. Half a dozen natives were moving about in front of the place, which appeared to be the only spot in the village with any activity.

"That must be where they took Tony," Joe said.

The trio rode to the end of the street and dismounted near the building. At first the natives paid little attention to them. But when Joe walked up to a man near the door and asked him in Spanish if he might go in and look around, the Indian scowled. He shook his head as if he did not understand Spanish and made a threatening gesture.

"Don't get tough," Joe said in English. "I'll just walk in."

"Careful, Joe!" Frank warned.

But his brother reached for the knob. At once two men stepped up, one on each side of the boy and struck him across the cheeks with the butt of their hard, bony hands. The force of the unexpected blows caused Joe to lose his balance and fall backward. Furious, he picked himself up and rushed at the bigger Indian, punching him soundly in the jaw.

"That was a beauty," Frank cried out.

The man's eyes glazed and his knees sagged, then he dropped with a half-turn to the porch.

"We'll take this one!" Frank yelled as he swept past Joe to meet the charge of the second man. Dodging a vicious blow, Frank swiftly crouched, grabbed his adversary's knees and hurled him to the floor. As he straightened up and turned to Joe, the doors of the building were flung wide open. Through the entrance swarmed the whole group of kidnappers.

Seeing their guards lying stunned on the floor, the angered Indians attacked the boys. The youths fought violently, but, being greatly outnumbered, were overwhelmed and quickly bound. Their captors, who had not spoken a word, led them through the doorway.

Inside, natives were carrying armfuls of mahogany wood to the center of the room. Other men sat silently in a circle. The building was not a shop after all, but some kind of ceremonial hall. Tony was not in sight. The captured boys were taken to the center of the circle.

"Look, they're starting a fire!" Chet's face turned white when an old man stepped forward from the circle and ignited the chips.

Standing inside the ring of about forty Indians who sat glowering at them, the Hardys whispered words of encouragement to each other and to Chet.

Some of the smoke was escaping through an opening in the roof, but the place was already hazy. The three boys began to cough.

"Maybe this is part of the curse that Willie Wortman warned us about!" Chet moaned. "We'll never get out of here alive!"

Frank, trying to keep up his courage, said he was afraid that the Indians had overheard them talking about the treasure. If this were the case and he could convince them that they did not intend to steal any of it, the boys might go free. But before Frank had a chance to try to speak up, Joe exclaimed, "Look what's happening now!"

The men in the circle began to chant on a single low note. Then two drummers entered the circle and started an accompaniment.

The sound of the beating drums grew louder. The men seated in the ring made rhythmic motions with their hands. The chanting increased in fervor—louder and louder, until the boys could no longer hear each other speak.

Snakelike, the circle came to life as the men, one by one, slowly rose to their feet and started stamping, sending clouds of dust swirling off the earth floor into the smoke-blue atmosphere.

At the entrance to the building stood four weirdly painted dancers wearing feathered headdresses. With a savage throbbing of the drums, these half-naked Indians, brandishing long spears, leaped into the moving circle of stamping fanatics.

As they whirled past the boys, the prisoners could see the milk-white and scarlet streaks of paint on the dancers' faces and the eerie blue lines daubed along their sweating shoulders.

"Kai-ee tamooka! Kai-ee tamooka!" the entire circle bellowed as the big dance got under way.

The solo dancers moved to the right as the circle stamped clockwise. Dust and smoke almost blinded the boys. The drummers started a faster beat. The chanting became a half-scream.

Then, as if by some invisible signal, the wild frenzy came to a sudden end. The performers stood as if frozen. Then a slow thump—thump—thumping of a lone drum began. Slowly the men in the circle re-formed their ring and crouched in silence on the dirt floor. A moment later the circle moved in on the boys and the dying fire.

Now the oldest man arose and approached the low-burning fire. With his arms extended, palms up, he stood for several moments without uttering a sound. Then, as several of the elder members of the circle began to murmur, the leader pulled a long stick from a sheath. With it he poked about in the embers. Scraping carefully, he heaped up a cone-shaped pile like those the boys had seen before!

The chanting ceased. The circle closed even smaller. The leader extended his arms a second time and the murmuring began again, a little louder than before. Now, with his stick, the man

The boys winced as the hot ashes struck their skin

scraped some of the warm ashes into a wooden bowl.

"*Kai-ee! Kai-ee!*" The chant picked up volume and the leader turned from the fire to face the Hardys and Chet. Holding the bowl out stiffly, chest high, he stopped directly in front of the boys. Inwardly quaking, the captives tried to appear unperturbed.

Murmuring the chant himself, the old Indian sprinkled the hot ashes on the foreheads of the trio. The boys winced but did not cry out.

There was a sudden commotion at the entrance. Then came a booming, commanding voice over the heads of the people. The leader, lowering the bowl, cried out:

"Tecum-Uman!"

The man for whom the boys had been searching! What would happen now?

CHAPTER XVIII

Into Dangerous Country

A handsome elderly Indian, taller than the other tribesmen, walked with stately steps toward the Hardys and Chet. He motioned to a native that they be unbound at once.

After this was done, the tall Indian addressed Frank in Spanish. "Do you speak this language?"

"A little," Frank replied, then hastened to ask, "Where is our friend? Is he all right?"

For the first time a faint smile played around the Indian's mouth. "He is quite safe. He is changing his clothes and will be brought here shortly. Your mules, also, are unharmed."

Frank told the boys this news, then said, "I don't understand what has happened, Tecum-Uman. We were advised to ask your aid by Señor Montero."

"Yes," the elderly man nodded. "The señor is an old friend of mine. I am sorry you have been poorly treated here."

Mystified, Frank asked him to explain the reasons for the odd happenings. Tecum-Uman motioned for the boys to follow him outside. Reaching a secluded spot, the man began to speak.

"I am chief of the three Kulkul villages," he said. "This is one of them but not where I live. I came here because certain men have been causing much trouble. They are the ones who captured young Prito and took you into the ceremonial hall."

Tecum-Uman explained that he was sure a certain dishonest Ladino in the area was responsible for the recent unrest in the village. "I believe he was the man who told my tribesmen that your friend was disguised as a shaman. This thing is regarded as a great evil by my people," he concluded. "The fire dance you witnessed is an old custom performed to break such a curse."

Frank said he regretted the misunderstanding. "Our reason for coming here," he told the chief, "is to find Texichapi. Do you know where it is?"

If the Kulkul chief was surprised by the question, he did not show it.

"Texichapi is reputed to be a day's journey west of the place where Prito said you were to get fresh mules and supplies." Tecum-Uman gave no further information. "You will be free to go with your friend when he arrives here. My loyal tribesmen wish you no harm."

As the old man concluded his statement, Tony was led toward them. Dressed in a blue cotton shirt and a pair of nondescript brown trousers, he rushed up to the boys.

"Am I glad to see you!" he cried. "I thought all of us were goners."

"So did we!" Chet exclaimed.

"Wait till you hear what happened to me," Tony whispered. "Tell you later."

There was no sign of the unfriendly natives as Tecum-Uman accompanied the boys to their mules. As a gesture of good will, he handed them a sack of food.

"You will arrive at the village where you change mules within one hour," Tecum-Uman said. "If you do not leave this trail, you cannot miss it."

The four travelers expressed hearty thanks for his help, and the elderly man waved good-by to them. As they rode away, the boys told Tony about their ordeal and about Tecum-Uman's explanation.

"He sure arrived in the nick of time," Joe said. "Now tell us what happened to you."

Tony sobered. "This shaman business was a fake," he said. "They knew right away I wasn't an Indian. What they wanted was to find out why we're here. They tried several torture tricks. I guess I can thank Tecum-Uman that things weren't any worse. He arrived in the midst of it.

But the guys that were holding me warned that if I told the chief anything, it would go badly with me later."

The Hardys were afraid that the group might be followed and urged their mules forward at a faster pace. Several times Frank dismounted and put his ear to the ground to detect any sounds of horsemen trailing them, but he heard nothing.

"I guess we're safe," he concluded.

Exactly as the old man had predicted, the boys arrived at the next village in one hour. They sought out the shopkeeper's relative who rented mules. He made arrangements for the group to remain overnight, and promised to have their mounts ready for an early-morning start. Frank told the man about Señor Montero's workers coming for the borrowed mules, and he promised to care for the animals until they arrived.

After buying fresh supplies, the boys were shown to the cabin where they were to sleep. The four agreed that they would ask no questions.

"We can't tell friend from foe in these mountains," Frank said, "so we'd better just be mum about the treasure."

Before the sun went down, the boys took a short walk around the trading post, inspecting the various supplies that were bought by traders, explorers, and settling farmers. Chet picked up a short-handled miner's shovel.

"Say, here's a tool we might need in Texichapi!" he exclaimed, breaking the silence concerning their destination.

An Indian standing nearby flashed a strange look at Chet. The boys expected him to vanish in the next instant and bring back reinforcements to harm them. But instead the man walked closer and spoke to them in broken Spanish.

"Texichapi?" he asked. "You going there?"

Since Chet had already given away their destination, the boys admitted that they were.

"Bad place," the Indian told them. "Stay away. It is valley of evil."

The man said that Texichapi was hard on a man physically because of its sudden and extreme changes in temperature. At times, the place was hot and damp. At other times the area was cold and swept by winds.

"And besides," he went on, "there are many mahogany trees in Texichapi which are protected by spirits. When someone not wanted tries to enter that section, a curse is put on him!"

The boys looked at one another, dismayed. But the part about the curse did not seem to ring true.

"Where did you learn about the curse?" Frank asked the Indian. But it seemed the man did not understand his stilted high school Spanish.

The Hardys and their friends tried to get the native to tell them whether this tale of the curse and the place being called the valley of evil was an old legend of the Indians or whether it was a recent one. It might be another stratagem of the boys' enemies, the patriotic society, to frighten away the quartet.

"No, sorry," the Indian replied.

Either he was pretending not to understand, or finding the language barrier between them was just too great.

The Indian drifted away and the boys returned to their cabin. All were uneasy about going to sleep, not knowing what might happen. But nothing disturbed them except the howling of wild animals in the nearby forest.

At the crack of dawn the group headed west as Tecum-Uman had instructed them. There was no indication that they were being followed. The boys pushed on and did not take a break in their difficult journey until the sun was directly overhead. Then they lunched briefly and set off again.

Much of the way seemed to be along dry river-beds and across streams which appeared to have left their former course to flow in adjacent ravines.

"There sure are a lot of crisscrossing trails," observed Frank, who was leading the cavalcade. "The trail to Texichapi would be mighty tough to follow if Tecum-Uman had not insisted that we keep heading straight west all the time."

Suddenly he stopped, and as the others waited, dismounted and picked up a stick. With it Frank scratched several marks in the dirt. Finishing the last line, he asked the others to look at what he had drawn. "Do these seem familiar?" he asked.

The boys studied the lines for only a few moments, then Joe exclaimed, "Of course. They're the ones on the medallions!"

Frank explained that he had traced the curves of the streams that they had just passed. "They exactly match the lines that we memorized! We must be in the middle of the Texichapi country!"

Joe looked around excitedly. "I wonder what the opal really meant—should we look for a certain tree, a cave, or maybe a particular hill?"

No one knew the answer. Taking their bearings on the curve of the last stream, the boys changed course slightly. For half a mile they made their way through swampy ground until they saw, sparkling like a jewel, a small lake at the base of a distant cliff.

"Do you think this lake corresponds to the location of the opal on the medallion?" asked Tony.

"I doubt that the treasure would be buried underwater," replied Frank. "Besides, we have to travel a little farther if my memory is correct."

The riders broke into a jog as the wooded countryside became more open. Within a few minutes they arrived at the lake.

"Look up there!" Joe cried suddenly.

Two figures stood at the top of a sheer wall of rock that dropped seventy or eighty feet straight down to the water. The sight of people in this apparently uninhabited area startled the boys. Could they be spies for the so-called patriotic society sent out to intercept them? But surely no spies would show themselves so plainly.

As the figures moved close to the rim of the cliff, the watchers could see that they were an Indian man and a small boy.

Frank was about to shout to the Indian when they saw the little boy break away from the man and run along the cliff's edge. They could hear the man give a warning shout. Abruptly the little boy turned to face the man, but lost his balance and hurtled toward the water.

The four gasped in horror as the small form struck the lake surface and disappeared. They realized that even if the youngster knew how to swim, a fall from such a height would knock the wind out of him and he would drown. The same would be true of the child's companion if he should dive in and attempt a rescue.

"I'm going after that boy!" Joe cried, slipping off his moccasins and jacket.

CHAPTER XIX

Followed!

As Joe dived into the lake, his friends watched apprehensively from the water's edge. There was still no sign of the boy who had fallen from the cliff.

"Perhaps it's already too late," Joe thought fearfully as he swam underwater.

Suddenly he saw the boy. His limp body was entangled in the branches of a sunken tree trunk. Relieved, but with the air in his lungs almost gone, Joe swam over and tried to release the unconscious boy. Just as he felt his lungs would burst, the branches gave way, and grasping the child firmly, he quickly rose to the surface.

As Joe emerged into the brilliant sunlight and inhaled great gulps of air, Frank cried out, "Great! Over here, Joe!"

His brother, still clutching the helpless child, headed for shore. As he drew near, Frank jumped into the water and said, "I'll take him!"

He reached for the little boy and carried him ashore. Joe followed. Frank laid the child on the ground and began to give him artificial respiration to force the water from his lungs. A few minutes later Chet took a turn, then Tony.

Presently the Indian who had been on the cliff appeared, tears streaming from his eyes. Jabbering in a language unintelligible to the boys and gesticulating, he indicated that the youngster was his son.

"He'll be all right," Frank said, noting that the child's pulse, though feeble, was picking up.

As water spewed from the little boy's mouth, his limbs began to twitch, and his breathing became more regular. Soon the child's eyes opened. Through gestures, Frank indicated to the Indian that his son was definitely out of danger, but should be put to bed for the rest of the day.

When the child was ready to travel, his father gently picked him up. The man, his face beaming with gratitude, nodded to each boy, then started homeward.

"That was a great rescue you made, Joe," Chet praised. "You've made a real friend of that Indian."

Joe removed his wet clothes. The warm breeze quickly dried them. After putting them back on, he said, "All set? Let's head for the treasure spot of Texichapi."

" 'The valley of evil,' " Chet quoted dolefully.

The four rode toward the place, which, according to the stranger at the trading center, had the power to cast an evil spell. After making two wrong turns, they finally came to an area which looked like the map on the medallions.

"It's beautiful here!" Tony exclaimed.

"Not windy and cold like that Indian said. And it certainly is cheerful," Chet remarked, watching the brilliantly colored birds in the trees.

Small clumps of spruce filled the valley, and as the mules moved silently over the pine-needled ground, the boys breathed in the crisp air.

"There's a big stand of mahogany trees ahead!" Frank said excitedly. "And that's the spot indicated on the map by the opal."

Eagerly they urged their mounts toward it. Reaching the grove of giant trees, Frank took a pad from his pocket and once more sketched all the lines from the medallions, including the precise location of the opal.

"Right here is where we start digging," he announced and marked the exact area. Then he tore the paper into small bits and scattered them in the breeze.

During the next five hours the boys dug without interruption. Nothing came to light. Finally, tired from the heavy work, they were about to quit for the day when Tony's pick hit a hard surface. It had struck rocks before, but this time there was a slightly different sound.

"Fellows," he said excitedly, "start shoveling here!" Working furiously the group gradually made out the shape of a stone step, then another leading into the earth.

"This is the beginning!" Joe cried. "Let's really dig!"

Into the dusk, then after a night's rest, all through the next morning, the quartet continued their excavation work. After uncovering a dozen steps with a carved balustrade, they came to a stone of a different type.

"This isn't a step," said Frank. "It's a slab laid across something."

They decided to pry the slab loose. This proved to be a backbreaking job, but at last they managed to upend the stone. Below it were more steps, almost free of earth.

Their hearts pounding, the boys beamed their lights ahead and descended. "I feel as if I were walking back through the centuries," Frank commented in a whisper.

In a few moments he and his companions found themselves standing in the anteroom of a huge building. "This must have been a palace!" Joe cried excitedly as his light picked up carved columns, benches, and walls.

Silently they made their way through richly carved reception rooms, altar rooms, and finally reached the vast throne room. Chet broke the stillness to exclaim, "Wowee! What a treasure!"

The frescoed walls and throne were of solid gold!

"Look at those chairs!" Tony gasped.

The carved seats were inlaid with varicolored woods. Opals and costly jade crowned the backs of each. Emeralds and rubies glistened from their settings in the golden throne. Eight-foot vases with mosaic figures of Aztec royalty filled the corners of the room.

"Whew!" Tony gasped. "I just don't believe I'm seeing all this. It must be a dream!"

"These treasures are certainly government property!" Frank said. "No one must be allowed to steal them. We must notify the Guatemalan government at once."

Retracing their steps, the boys saw one entire room filled with golden figures.

"Why, this one room alone is worth a fortune!" Joe exclaimed. "No wonder Torres and Valez were ready to kill us to obtain the medallions."

Passing through the reception room hung with tapestries of golden thread woven through the brilliant plumage of tropical birds, the boys approached the steps.

"It seems darker here than when we came down," Tony remarked.

The reason soon became obvious to the boys. Several shadowy forms were standing guard at the entrance! Some of them were the boys' tormentors from the Kulkul village, others were white men, including a tall, blond fellow.

"The kitchen gadget salesman Callie told us about!" shot through Joe's mind.

"They've followed us here," Frank whispered. "Even the masquerading 'woman' from the plane!" he groaned. "I recognize his face."

The man stepped forward. He introduced himself as Alberto Torres, leader of the "patriots."

"I am glad to see the detectives from the States. Of course it will be impossible for you to escape," he added. "Permit me to thank you for leading us to the treasure we have sought for so long."

As Frank started to reply, one of the surly-looking guards slapped him across the mouth.

Torres went on, "And now that the fabled treasure has been located, we have no time to lose. You boys will be sealed inside this palace to die while we go for more equipment."

Led by Frank, the four prisoners bolted for the steps, knocking over several of the guards. But the Hardys and their friends were blocked at the bottom step.

"Do not act foolish," Torres warned them, "or you will die sooner."

The power he held over the boys suddenly inflated his ego. "I fooled you all, you and your father," he boasted. "That Valez—he was stupid to let himself get caught. And Willie Wortman is dumb too. He sells the medallions—the key to this treasure."

"Where did the medallions come from?" Frank spoke up.

The guard was about to strike him again, but Torres raised his hand in a swaggering motion to stop him. "I can at least amuse you before you die by answering some of your questions," the pompous leader replied. "To begin with, those medallions were cleverly and secretly made by an old Kulkul Indian who had wandered away from his tribe. Most likely he had discovered the treasure and made the medallions as a future guide for Tecum-Uman. He died suddenly in the forest and Wortman's buddy found them on the body of the old Indian. He showed them to me. When I realized later that they must be of great value, I tried to get them from Wortman's friend. But he had disappeared.

"I sent Luis Valez," he continued, "to find him. He learned Willie Wortman had received the coins in the meantime and had sold them to Roberto Prito in New York. Valez went there, then on to Bayport. Willie Wortman, meanwhile, had begun to suspect something, and he too began to search for the medallions."

"Were you the man who got away from me in New York?" Joe interrupted.

"I was," Torres replied boastfully. "When Valez seemed to be failing in his mission," he continued, "I hunted up Willie Wortman in New York. I was following him that day when you saw us. I didn't find out anything from him, so I went to Bayport to check on Valez. He was in jail and I learned you were coming to Guatemala, so I boarded the same flight. You got away at the New York airport, but I took the next plane here."

Torres's statement that he had arrived in Bayport after his henchman's arrest cleared up one of the questions in the minds of the Hardys. He was not the man who had helped Valez when he had waylaid Joe and stolen the opal medallion.

"How did you find out we were coming to Guatemala?" Frank asked.

"I learned about it from a friend at the consulate in New York. The patriotic society kept track of you. They traced you through a Guatemala City taxi company and found that you were already headed out here to the hills."

"Did you arrange what happened to us at the fire ceremony?" Frank queried.

"Yes. And one of my spies tried to keep you from this place by telling you it is a valley of evil."

After a pause, Torres added, "Tecum-Uman hates me, but I have many friends. I sent word to them to bring you in. The old man knew nothing of this. But when he showed up he was told a story of his people having to break a curse you had brought them because of a false shaman."

"You didn't plan on our leaving that village," Joe said.

"No. I was going to get the truth out of you

about the treasure right there. But it does not matter. You found it for us, anyway."

"It's too bad that Tecum-Uman doesn't have a loyal following in all his villages," Frank said. "He'd drive a thief like you out of the country!"

"No more talk like that," Torres retorted angrily, "or I won't even bother to seal you in! I'll kill you right now!"

Frank, stalling for time and hoping that the boys could think of a way to outwit Torres, questioned the vain man again.

"Luis Valez is good with a blowgun, isn't he?"

"Very good. Learned it from a South American Indian."

"Tell me about the first medallion he stole."

Torres whirled around. "You say Valez stole it?"

"Yes. He and his friend, whoever he is!"

"That dirty double-crosser!" Torres roared. "He was playing his own game and must still have the coin!"

In spite of Frank's attempt to continue the conversation, Torres, ruffled by the news of Valez's betrayal, suddenly shouted, "Enough of this delay! Seal these four in!"

He headed for the steps, and without looking back, disappeared onto the ground level. The six guards closed in!

CHAPTER XX

The Secret Revealed

KNOWING that they were doomed to certain death in the buried palace if they could not elude the guards, the Hardys, Tony, and Chet realized they must make a desperate attempt.

"Our only chance is to slug it out with them," whispered Frank.

Quickly the boys retreated to the middle of the room and braced themselves for the attack. Two of the enemy headed for Joe, who ducked, grabbed one native's arm, and swiftly slung him jujitsu fashion over his shoulder. The man crashed against a heavy stone idol and lay dazed. Joe's second opponent caught the boy square on the chest and the two fell, rolling over and over.

Chet, knocked to the floor by a husky Indian, decided to use strategy. As the native above him closed in, the boy pretended to let himself be taken. The man relaxed and motioned for Chet to stand up. As he rose, Chet brought the back of his head up flush under the jaw of the unsuspecting enemy, who at once collapsed.

"Two down—four to go!" cried Chet, running toward Tony who was being backed into a corner.

Chet reached out with both hands and caught the coarse black hair of the man nearest him. Tony did the same to another man. With a quick, jerking motion the boys banged the skulls of the natives together with such a crack that the two dropped in a heap, unconscious.

Joe was still struggling with his man, and Frank was being beaten by the biggest of the attacking group.

"Come on, Chet!" yelled Tony, racing across the room. With only two natives left to subdue, they had a chance for escape!

But just then six more Indians swarmed down the steps. There was nothing for the boys to do but surrender. They were lashed tightly, then laid at the foot of the steps.

The bandits were jubilant! Shouting words of self-praise, they started up the steps. Suddenly, in the bright light of the opening, an Indian with drawn bow appeared. He let fly with the arrow. One of the bandits screamed in pain as the flint arrowhead seared into his raised right arm. He crumpled to his knees, begging the Indian not to release the second arrow, which was already aimed at him.

Several Indians came running down the steps

after their leader. Herding the boys' captors into a corner, they ordered one of them to release Frank and Tony from their bonds, who in turn freed Joe and Chet.

"We're mighty glad to see you!" Frank said. "But where did you come from?"

"Kulkul village," the man replied, pointing to the steps. The boys turned to look. At the top of the stairs stood the father of the little boy Joe had rescued!

The quartet rushed up to thank the man. He asked one of his friends to act as interpreter.

"He say after you save boy he see you go on path to Texichapi. He start to worry," the man began. "He know we have some bad people in one Kulkul village. When he see them after you, he run to loyal Kulkuls and tell us come quick with him."

"We want to thank you and all the loyal Kulkuls for saving our lives," Frank said.

"Tomas, the boy's father, he say we equal," the man replied. "You save his son. We save you."

A moment later they saw Tecum-Uman approaching. He told them that Torres and his gang were under guard, adding that he had already sent a messenger to inform the officials.

"You have done a noble act for the Guatemalan government," the old man said to Frank as he excitedly started on a tour through the palace with the discoverers.

"Yes," the interpreter added, "place belong to

ancestor. Thank you for find. Nobody steal. Sacred for government fathers."

"I wonder what Torres is thinking about now," Chet remarked. "I'll bet he's not boasting!"

"We'll find out after we come back from showing Tecum-Uman and his friends the rest of the palace," Frank replied.

The boys led the way through the wealth and beauty of the rooms. The Indians were overcome with joy as they saw the splendor of their earlier civilization. Tears of happiness filled Tecum-Uman's eyes.

"With Torres arrested and in jail," the old man said, "the Kulkul tribe will become united again. And this wonderful palace can be restored. The tribal gods have looked on us with favor."

As they moved along, playing their flashlights from one priceless object to another, Chet, who had been leaning against a jewel-paneled wall, suddenly cried, "Hey, what's this?" as the panel swung open. "A whole new passageway!"

Eagerly the boys beamed their lights into this area. On their previous trip they had thought the decorated rectangle was part of a solid wall.

Tecum-Uman and the others accompanied them into the newly found section. The old man's eyes glistened as he explained to the boys that this must have been a sacred ceremonial room. It was fashioned of pale-pink granite, which probably had been transported from South America,

Tecum-Uman said. Here, too, were costly idols made of beautifully carved woods, silver, or gold set with precious jewels.

"See this!" Joe called to the others. "We could adopt it as the souvenir of our discovery."

As he flashed his light on a head ornament mounted on the wall, the group saw a large central figure of a god surrounded by four human figures.

"You mean Tecum-Uman in middle and four boys from States!" the old man said, smiling.

The inspection ended, the group retraced their way through the palace and climbed the steps to the surface. Across a small clearing the notorious Torres, guarded by several Indians, stood staring glumly at the ground. At the sight of the boys, the leader of the criminals flew into a rage.

"I will get my revenge!" he yelled. In spite of the Kulkuls' efforts to silence him, he continued screaming at the boys.

"Say, Torres," Chet called, "next time you impersonate a woman, remember to wear gloves— your hands gave you away!"

Torres, incensed by Chet's remark, clenched his large fists and kept shouting. But a moment later, when reinforcements of loyal Kulkuls ran into the clearing, the man became silent. Tecum-Uman told the boys not to worry about further trouble with Torres and his gang.

Posting a guard at the entrance to the palace,

the tribal chief asked the boys to get their mules and walk with him at the head of a procession back to the nearby Kulkul village.

"You are heroes," he said, "and my people will want to thank you. But tell me how you learned of this treasure."

The Hardys explained about the medallions and Torres. When they finished the story, Tecum-Uman nodded his head. He said that an elderly member of his tribe had been taken ill while on a hunting trip and died before he could get back to his village. The old man probably was the Indian from whom Willie Wortman's sailor friend had gotten the medallions.

After packing the rented equipment, the boys joined Tecum-Uman. Amidst the cheers of the Kulkuls, the parade started.

The exciting news of the Hardys' discovery of the long-buried palace and the arrest of the law-breaker Torres turned the sleepy village into a buzzing beehive. Everywhere the usually silent natives talked excitedly about the news that trickled in ahead of the heroes.

"Tecum-Uman, he say big celebration to honor four boys," a panting messenger had told the villagers, running from house to house.

Immediately all of the Indians' bright-colored finery was brought out. Women adorned themselves in gay festival dresses and prepared great dishes of food for the banquet.

Meanwhile, the menfolk had built fires in the barbecue pits and started roasting chunks of tender beef and pork on the turning spits. The children linked fresh flowers into streamers and strung them above the entrance to the village. Each cottage flew the Guatemalan flag. Musicians tuned up their primitive instruments and awaited the arrival of the heroes. By the time the Hardys arrived with Chet and Tony, everything was ready.

"Smell that!" Chet said, sniffing the delicious aroma of the roasting meat. "It must be true that we're going to have a feast. I can't wait!"

The native band started playing as the boys looked around, smiling. To the cheers of the Indians, the visitors were escorted to a low, decorated table in the public square.

Young Indian girls passed huge dishes of fruits, maize, beans, and meat.

During the meal Tecum-Uman told the boys that he had already sent word to the Guatemalan president requesting that each of them be given a gold souvenir from the buried palace as a token of his country's gratefulness.

"We don't expect a reward," said Joe. "We've had a grand time visiting your beautiful country."

The old chief looked pleased.

The Hardys and their friends remained in the village for the next two days. Finally federal officers arrived to take the prisoners. And with them was a grinning Jorge Almeida, bearing a large white envelope.

Jorge hopped off the mule he was riding. "You heroes, *amigos!*" he cried. "Why you not tell me you look for this treasure? Never would I go back to the city!"

After explaining why secrecy had been important, Tony asked how Jorge had learned about the treasure.

"Why, all the papers tell about the great thing you did," the man said excitedly.

Then Jorge told how he had personally called on the president and related his part in the adventure. When he had requested permission to come out and see the treasure, the president had said that he could accompany the police and deliver the letter he now carried.

"It is for all of you," he said, handing the envelope to Joe. The letter, signed with the president's name, thanked the boys for the discovery and requested that they each take home a souvenir.

Later that afternoon the four Americans and Jorge journeyed to the ancient site with Tecum-Uman. While the chief led Jorge through the palace rooms, the boys decided on what souvenirs they would choose.

Chet picked up a large, jeweled bowl. "This must be what the king used for his special dinners," he said. "It's just the thing for me!"

"Are you sure it's big enough?" Joe quipped with a grin.

Chet made a face. "I can always use it as a dessert bowl."

A delicately carved bracelet of gold was Frank's choice. He knew his mother would like it.

"And I'll take this for Aunt Gertrude," Joe decided, picking up a small golden idol. "It may even try to talk back to her!"

As Tony selected an ancient, gold-encrusted bow and arrow, he said, "On our way home let's stop in New York and see Willie Wortman. Those medallions have served their purpose and I'll give him the one I have."

"This way the curse is broken!" Joe grinned.

"For a while it really looked as if there was a curse on them," Frank agreed.

For a short time the Hardys were to be free of a mystery. Then another, called *The Secret of Pirates' Hill,* was to come their way and involve Frank and Joe in a series of harrowing and dangerous experiences. But at the moment this was far from their thoughts.

"This place hokay!" Jorge exclaimed when he joined the boys. His eyes sparkling, he added, "I would not mind living in luxury like this!"

Joe laughed. "You're too busy driving your taxi!"

"Oh, yes. You must see my new one! The horn,

she is like music. I park her back at trading village. We pick her up and you ride to city with me?"

"Sure. But how about that volcano? The road must still be blocked," Joe said.

Jorge grinned. "I find new way!"

Order Form
Own the original 56 thrilling
NANCY DREW MYSTERY STORIES®

In *hardcover* at your local bookseller OR
simply mail in this handy order coupon and start your collection today!

Please send me the following Nancy Drew titles I've checked below.
All Books Priced @ $5.99

AVOID DELAYS Please Print Order Form Clearly

❑	1	Secret of the Old Clock	448-09501-7	❑ 30	Clue of the Velvet Mask	448-09530-0
❑	2	Hidden Staircase	448-09502-5	❑ 31	Ringmaster's Secret	448-09531-9
❑	3	Bungalow Mystery	448-09503-3	❑ 32	Scarlet Slipper Mystery	448-09532-7
❑	4	Mystery at Lilac Inn	448-09504-1	❑ 33	Witch Tree Symbol	448-09533-5
❑	5	Secret of Shadow Ranch	448-09505-X	❑ 34	Hidden Window Mystery	448-09534-3
❑	6	Secret of Red Gate Farm	448-09506-8	❑ 35	Haunted Showboat	448-09535-1
❑	7	Clue in the Diary	448-09507-6	❑ 36	Secret of the Golden Pavilion	448-09536-X
❑	8	Nancy's Mysterious Letter	448-09508-4	❑ 37	Clue in the Old Stagecoach	448-09537-8
❑	9	The Sign of the Twisted Candles	448-09509-2	❑ 38	Mystery of the Fire Dragon	448-09538-6
❑	10	Password to Larkspur Lane	448-09510-6	❑ 39	Clue of the Dancing Puppet	448-09539-4
❑	11	Clue of the Broken Locket	448-09511-4	❑ 40	Moonstone Castle Mystery	448-09540-8
❑	12	The Message in the Hollow Oak	448-09512-2	❑ 41	Clue of the Whistling Bagpipes	448-09541-6
❑	13	Mystery of the Ivory Charm	448-09513-0	❑ 42	Phantom of Pine Hill	448-09542-4
❑	14	The Whispering Statue	448-09514-9	❑ 43	Mystery of the 99 Steps	448-09543-2
❑	15	Haunted Bridge	448-09515-7	❑ 44	Clue in the Crossword Cipher	448-09544-0
❑	16	Clue of the Tapping Heels	448-09516-5	❑ 45	Spider Sapphire Mystery	448-09545-9
❑	17	Mystery of the Brass-Bound Trunk	448-09517-3	❑ 46	The Invisible Intruder	448-09546-7
❑	18	Mystery at Moss-Covered Mansion	448-09518-1	❑ 47	The Mysterious Mannequin	448-09547-5
❑	19	Quest of the Missing Map	448-09519-X	❑ 48	The Crooked Banister	448-09548-3
❑	20	Clue in the Jewel Box	448-09520-3	❑ 49	The Secret of Mirror Bay	448-09549-1
❑	21	The Secret in the Old Attic	448-09521-1	❑ 50	The Double Jinx Mystery	448-09550-5
❑	22	Clue in the Crumbling Wall	448-09522-X	❑ 51	Mystery of the Glowing Eye	448-09551-3
❑	23	Mystery of the Tolling Bell	448-09523-8	❑ 52	The Secret of the Forgotten City	448-09552-1
❑	24	Clue in the Old Album	448-09524-6	❑ 53	The Sky Phantom	448-09553-X
❑	25	Ghost of Blackwood Hall	448-09525-4	❑ 54	The Strange Message	
❑	26	Clue of the Leaning Chimney	448-09526-2		in the Parchment	448-09554-8
❑	27	Secret of the Wooden Lady	448-09527-0	❑ 55	Mystery of Crocodile Island	448-09555-6
❑	28	The Clue of the Black Keys	448-09528-9	❑ 56	The Thirteenth Pearl	448-09556-4
❑	29	Mystery at the Ski Jump	448-09529-7			

VISIT PENGUIN PUTNAM BOOKS FOR YOUNG READERS ONLINE:
http://www.penguinputnam.com/yreaders/index.htm

Payable in US funds only. Postage & handling: US/Can. $2.75 for one book, $1.00 for each add'l book not to exceed $6.75; Int'l $5.00 for one book, $1.00 for each add'l. We accept Visa, MC, AMEX ($10.00 min.), checks ($15.00 fee for returned checks), and money orders. No Cash/COD. Call (800) 788-6262 or (201) 933-9292, fax (201) 896-8569, or mail your orders to:

Penguin Putnam Inc.   Bill my
PO Box 12289 Dept. B   credit card # _____ exp.____
Newark, NJ 07101-5289   ___ Visa ___ MC ___ AMEX
                                Signature: _____

Bill to: _____   Book Total $_____
Address _____
City _____ ST _____ ZIP_____   Applicable sales tax $_____
Daytime phone #_____
                                                Postage & Handling $_____
Ship to:_____
Address_____   Total amount due $_____
City _____ ST _____ ZIP_____

Please allow 4–6 weeks for US delivery. Can./Int'l orders please allow 6–8 weeks.
This offer is subject to change without notice.   Ad # _____